Killer in the Window NOV 1 7 2009

The modified Colt bucked against Clint's palm, sending two quick shots up to the window across the street. He wasn't sure who else was in that second-floor room, so he did his best to be as accurate as possible. Both bullets found their mark without shattering any glass or even nicking a window frame.

The rifleman jerked up and back as hot lead ripped through him. His finger clenched around the trigger to send a wild shot into the large wood sign directly over Pace's main entrance. . .

DON'T MISS THESE
ALL-ACTION WESTERN SERIES
FROM THE BERKLEY PUBLISHING GROUP

THE GUNSMITH by J. R. Roberts
Clint Adams was a legend among lawmen, outlaws, and ladies. They called him . . . the Gunsmith.

LONGARM by Tabor Evans
The popular long-running series about Deputy U.S. Marshal Custis Long—his life, his loves, his fight for justice.

SLOCUM by Jake Logan
Today's longest-running action Western. John Slocum rides a deadly trail of hot blood and cold steel.

BUSHWHACKERS by B. J. Lanagan
An action-packed series by the creators of Longarm! The rousing adventures of the most brutal gang of cutthroats ever assembled—Quantrill's Raiders.

DIAMONDBACK by Guy Brewer
Dex Yancey is Diamondback, a Southern gentleman turned con man when his brother cheats him out of the family fortune. Ladies love him. Gamblers hate him. But nobody pulls one over on Dex . . .

WILDGUN by Jack Hanson
The blazing adventures of mountain man Will Barlow—from the creators of Longarm!

TEXAS TRACKER by Tom Calhoun
J.T. Law: the most relentless—and dangerous—manhunter in all Texas. Where sheriffs and posses fail, he's the best man to bring in the most vicious outlaws—for a price.

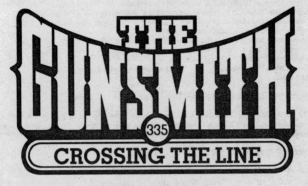

THE GUNSMITH

335

CROSSING THE LINE

J. R. ROBERTS

JOVE BOOKS, NEW YORK

THE BERKLEY PUBLISHING GROUP
Published by the Penguin Group
Penguin Group (USA) Inc.
375 Hudson Street, New York, New York 10014, USA
Penguin Group (Canada), 90 Eglinton Avenue East, Suite 700, Toronto, Ontario M4P 2Y3, Canada
(a division of Pearson Penguin Canada Inc.)
Penguin Books Ltd., 80 Strand, London WC2R 0RL, England
Penguin Group Ireland, 25 St. Stephen's Green, Dublin 2, Ireland (a division of Penguin Books Ltd.)
Penguin Group (Australia), 250 Camberwell Road, Camberwell, Victoria 3124, Australia
(a division of Pearson Australia Group Pty. Ltd.)
Penguin Books India Pvt. Ltd., 11 Community Centre, Panchsheel Park, New Delhi—110 017, India
Penguin Group (NZ), 67 Apollo Drive, Rosedale, North Shore 0632, New Zealand
(a division of Pearson New Zealand Ltd.)
Penguin Books (South Africa) (Pty.) Ltd., 24 Sturdee Avenue, Rosebank, Johannesburg 2196,
South Africa

Penguin Books Ltd., Registered Offices: 80 Strand, London WC2R 0RL, England

This is a work of fiction. Names, characters, places, and incidents either are the product of the author's imagination or are used fictitiously, and any resemblance to actual persons, living or dead, business establishments, events, or locales is entirely coincidental.

CROSSING THE LINE

A Jove Book / published by arrangement with the author

PRINTING HISTORY
Jove edition / November 2009

Copyright © 2009 by Robert J. Randisi.
Cover illustration by Sergio Giovine.

ISBN: 978-0-515-14707-0

JOVE®
Jove Books are published by The Berkley Publishing Group,
a division of Penguin Group (USA) Inc.,
375 Hudson Street, New York, New York 10014.
JOVE® is a registered trademark of Penguin Group (USA) Inc.
The "J" design is a trademark of Penguin Group (USA) Inc.

PRINTED IN THE UNITED STATES OF AMERICA

10 9 8 7 6 5 4 3 2 1

ONE

Pace's Emporium wasn't the best place Clint had ever played cards, but it was the finest establishment of its kind in town. Considering that the town in question was Trickle Creek, Kansas, that wasn't saying much. Built around a pair of mills that had been shut down after a rockslide choked off the town's main water supply, Trickle Creek had carried on well enough. There were railroad tracks not too far away, a well-used trail bringing travelers straight down Main Street, and enough drinking going on to keep most of the local saloons flush for a long time.

Clint had intended on riding through Trickle Creek without much thought, but Eclipse had other ideas. The Darley Arabian stallion began fretting as soon as he caught sight of civilization. At first, Clint figured the big fella was thirsty. After stopping in front of a trough, Clint had climbed down from the saddle to let him drink. When Eclipse didn't so much as flick his tongue into the water, Clint guessed he was hungry for something other than what he could get from grazing. Leading the stallion to a stable forced Clint to venture a bit further away from Main Street.

If Eclipse had wanted to trick Clint into staying in town, the plan had worked perfectly. The smell of a hot meal perked Clint's interest, and a sign advertising a local poker tournament held that interest even longer. Clint put the Darley Arabian up for the night at the livery and even paid extra for some good greens. Eclipse pulled his weight more than enough, so Clint figured he owed it to the stallion to indulge him every now and then. Besides, there was plenty in Trickle Creek to keep Clint busy for a day or two.

Before sundown that first day, Clint had found Pace's Emporium. By that same evening, he'd made it to a lucrative little game being played there. A little ways past midnight, he'd caught the eye of a tall brunette dealing Faro at one of the tables lining the perimeter of Pace's main room.

Judging by the crowd around her table, Clint realized he wasn't the first one to spot the pretty dealer. When she stood up to shake winners' hands or wave to someone else in the place, she proved to be taller than a good portion of the men surrounding her table. Her dark red dress clung to a trim yet shapely body, which she displayed proudly. Clint caught her sweeping her long hair over her shoulder just to make sure the players got a look at the ample cleavage shown by her dress's low-cut neckline. More than once, she'd snapped her eyes up to catch Clint watching her from across the room. When that happened, she flashed him a warm smile followed by a playful wag of her finger.

"You watching this game or the one over there?" one of the men at Clint's table asked.

The man to Clint's left turned to look toward the faro tables and then chuckled. "He's just watching Delilah work her magic, is all."

The first one to cut into Clint's line of sight sat directly across from him. He didn't need to twist around to get a look at the pretty dealer. "Him and every other man in this place. Ain't none of you ever seen a woman before?"

"What's the matter, George?" the man to Clint's left grunted. "Has it been a while since you seen one?"

While everyone else at the table found that amusing,

George obviously didn't. "You wanna dip your wick into some whore? Go do it. You wanna play cards? Stop gawking and do it!"

While he may have cracked the first joke, the man to Clint's left was the first to stop laughing. "Delilah ain't a whore," he snarled as he began getting to his feet.

Reaching out to nudge the other man back into his chair, Clint said, "Forget about it, Jack. He's right. We're here to play poker, and it's my turn to bet."

Jack looked to be about twenty years Clint's senior, but he wasn't some frail codger. The wrinkles under his eyes were more like cracks etched into stone and the gray dusted throughout his bushy hair made him look weathered instead of just plain old. Although he could have easily pushed himself all the way up, Jack allowed himself to drop back onto his chair. "Guess I'll let it slide," he grumbled.

The man directly across from Clint smirked as if he'd won a major battle. Unable to let a sleeping dog lie, he mumbled, "Damn right, you will."

There were two others sitting at the table that hadn't spoken up yet. One was a skinny banker named Wendell, and the other was big enough to make the chair beneath him look like a poorly constructed toy. The other men called him Bull. It wasn't the most original nickname, but it was appropriate.

"That's enough of that," Bull said. "We ain't here to gawk at women, and we ain't here to kick up trouble."

"Fine by me," Clint said.

"What about you, George?"

Grudgingly, the man across from Clint nodded. "I guess."

Since that was the best truce he could expect, Clint looked down at the two pair he was holding and shoved in a five-dollar bet.

Without taking his eyes off of George, Jack said, "Call."

"Five to me, huh?" George asked. "That's the best you could do? Make it ten."

Bull sighed, glanced at his cards, and promptly folded them.

Just then, Clint noticed the pretty faro dealer again. Unlike the last few times, he hadn't watched her just because she was a fine-looking woman in a formfitting dress. Instead, she'd caught his attention because she'd been staring at him with enough intensity for Clint to feel it from all the way across the room. When he met her gaze, he saw her shake her head.

"Ten?" Wendell groused. "Did you make a hand for yourself after all?"

"One way to find out," George told the banker. "Call or fold."

Letting out a pained groan, Wendell plainly wanted to fold. However, since he'd been the one to make the initial bet, he found it difficult to abandon his investment so easily. When he placed the correct number of chips in the pot, he might as well have been handing over one of his own children.

Clint had played plenty of poker in his years. He knew when another man was posturing because he had a real hand and when he was just trying to look strong. At the moment, George struck him as a man who was impatient and making a bet just to save face after being scolded by Bull. His intention had been to raise, just to push George out or soak him for a few extra dollars. When he touched his chips, Clint got another searing gaze from the faro dealer.

George sat as he always did, leaning one elbow against the table and holding his cards in a wide fan. "What's the matter, Adams? Too rich for ya? Maybe you'd like to ask that whore you fancy so much?"

"She ain't a whore!" Jack roared.

Clint couldn't figure out what was bothering the dealer, but she shook her head fiercely. He must have been staring a bit too hard at her, because George realized where Clint was looking and twisted around to see for himself. A split second before George was facing her, the dealer shifted her attention to one of the players at her own table.

"What is it?" George asked. "What the hell's got you so distracted?"

Before another ruckus could get going, Clint shoved in some chips. "See your raise and bump it up another twenty."

It wasn't a big raise to a professional gambler, but was more than enough to make some waves in a pond as small as this one. Jack threw in his cards as if they'd burned his fingers, but George called. Bull was already out and Wendell was next to drop, leaving Clint and George as the last men standing.

"Well?" George asked smugly. "What've you got?"

Clint showed his two pair. "Queens and nines."

"Three aces!" George announced as he raked in the pot. "Bite down on 'em!"

Clint looked across the room to the faro table to find the pretty dealer shaking her head and shrugging in a manner that practically screamed "I told you so."

TWO

It was well past two in the morning, but Clint's poker game was still going strong. The only one of the players to show any sign of slowing down was Wendell, but that only amounted to a lot of yawning in between hands. Bull always looked half asleep and Jack was drinking enough cheap whiskey to fuel a furnace.

George sat behind a pile of chips bigger than anyone else's at the table, which included a pocket watch and a tarnished pair of cuff links. Clint decided that the other man wasn't so much a good bluffer as he was a smug pain in the ass. He was always an asshole, which made it difficult to tell when he was putting on a show or just being himself.

As far as Clint could tell, George acted like a prick when he had a hand and acted like an even bigger one when he didn't. On the occasions when Clint had beaten him, George acted like a prick because he'd lost. After a few hours of that, it became tough for Clint to tell one level of smugness from another. There was, however, one peculiar element that kept him intrigued. That element was still dealing faro from the other side of the room.

Every so often, Clint would still get either a frown or a smirk from her. Sometimes those expressions were accompanied by a nod or a shake of her head. Sometimes, those were aimed at other players instead of at Clint. It took a while, but he eventually realized when the dealer was looking at him and when she wasn't. Even more importantly, he'd figured out just what all those nods and shakes actually meant.

George threw in a bet, which was called by Bull. Wendell folded, leaving the next decision up to Clint.

Since the faro game across the room was on an upswing, the dealer was preoccupied. Clint called and then waited for his replacement cards to be dealt. In that time, a few faro players bickered about something or other, which allowed the dealer to shift her eyes in Clint's direction.

When he looked at the two cards he'd been dealt to replace the ones he'd tossed, George smirked. Unfortunately, it was one of the same toothy smirks he always showed when he wasn't cussing at someone. "Fifteen dollars," George grunted as he threw in his chips.

Bull surveyed the table, glanced at his cards, looked around, and then looked at his cards again.

"They ain't changin'," George snapped. Although cowed by the fire in Bull's eyes, George still muttered, "Well they ain't."

"Fold," Bull declared. Not only did he lay down his cards, but he also stood up and added, "I'm going home."

"What?" George asked. "You still got some of my money!"

"I won it."

"Yeah, and a man should have a chance to win it back!"

"You've had plenty of chances," Bull declared. He then tipped his hat to the rest of the table and walked away.

Gritting his teeth, George said, "Someone should teach him some proper card table manners."

"Really?" Clint chuckled as he reached for his chips. From the corner of his eye, he spotted the dealer standing up and leaning forward. While her own players were content to gaze down the front of her dress, she was gazing across at him and shaking her head.

As much as Clint wanted to keep George from pulling in another pot right then and there, he laid down his cards.

"You fold?" George asked.

Clint nodded. "That's right."

"You can't fold."

"Why not?"

"The man wants to fold, let him fold," Jack grumbled.

"What about you, old man?" George asked. "In or out?"

"I suppose I'm out."

George nodded solemnly as he pulled in the pot and snarled, "Best hand I get all night and there ain't nobody with the balls to play the hand with me."

"Eh, go stuff yerself," the older man grumbled as he dealt the next hand.

Betting commenced, which George bumped up to a slightly higher level than normal. Clint stayed in the game after answering a few modest raises. After pitching one card to fill a straight, he only got a six to pair the one he'd been originally dealt.

"Twenty-five," George announced as he shoved in some money.

The faro dealer was watching the game intently and she displayed a wide smile that was obviously intended for Clint. Not one to disappoint a lady, Clint put in a twenty dollar raise.

"Too rich for my blood," Jack said.

"Raise?" George asked.

"You heard me," Clint replied.

Putting on another one of his smug grins, George shrugged and shoved in even more money. "Then I suppose I'll have to raise it again. Make it another eighty."

Clint's instincts told him that George didn't have what it took to bluff away such a generous portion of his stack. The dealer's wide smile, on the other hand, told him he might just have a bad read on the man across from him. Reluctantly, Clint pushed in all of his remaining funds to cover the bet.

"You sure you want to do that?" George asked.

"Too late to fix it now."

"This is a gentleman's game. You can take it back if you made a mistake."

Now, Clint felt like an idiot for giving George any credit whatsoever. "Since when have you conducted this as a gentleman's game? I've got a pair of sixes."

Even after Clint showed his hand, George couldn't believe it. "Sixes? You call me with a pair of sixes? What kind of damn fool play is that?"

"Something tells me it's a winning play. Care to prove me wrong?"

"I ain't got nothin' to prove!"

"Sure you do," Clint said. "Prove you can beat a pair of sixes."

George didn't show his cards, but he slapped them down with almost enough force to splinter the table. "You're cheatin'."

"What did you say?"

"How the hell did you know what I had?" Before anyone could answer that question, George twisted around in his seat and turned toward the smiling faro dealer. "It was that black son of a bitch, wasn't it?"

"Huh?"

"That's the same bastard that tried to cheat me at faro. Now he's tryin' to get back at me by helpin' you cheat at poker!"

Clint had to look around a few times before he could figure out what the hell George was talking about. Then, he picked out one black man seated next to the pretty dealer at the end of the faro table, where he handed out winnings and collected markers throughout the game.

"What kind of bullshit are you talking about?" Jack asked.

Nodding furiously, George stood up and reached for the gun at his hip. "I won't be cheated by the same man twice, and I sure as hell won't allow some black son of a bitch to make a fool out of me!"

"Sit down and shut yer trap," Jack said. "You're makin' a big enough fool outta yourself."

But Clint knew George wasn't listening to any of that. The time for talk had passed. If Clint didn't do something pretty damn quickly, the black man assisting the tall brunette wouldn't have much time left to draw another breath.

THREE

George kicked his chair away and stalked toward the faro table. "You think you can cheat me, boy? Twice?" He had yet to draw his pistol, but his fingers were wrapped around its grip tightly enough to turn his knuckles white.

The black man sitting at the faro table scooted away and looked around for the one who'd set George off. Quickly realizing he was the target for the other man's angry stare, he squared his shoulders to George and extended his arms to either side. "I don't want any trouble."

"Well, you signed up for plenty of trouble when you decided to swindle me outta my hard-earned money!" Suddenly, George was stopped by a hand that slapped down upon his shoulder.

"He didn't swindle you out of anything, George," Clint said from directly behind the angry man.

Struggling to break from Clint's grasp, George grunted, "You'll get yours soon enough."

"If you're angry about how that hand turned out, then take it up with me." Since he wasn't taken up on that offer right away, Clint spun George around to face him. "Or are you too certain that I'll clean your clock for making that accusation?"

Now that he was looking Clint dead in the eyes, George picked him as his new target. "All right, then. You cheated me outta my money."

Clint kept a straight face, but had to work hard to keep it that way. Technically speaking, George had a point. Although George obviously didn't know all the details, Clint had gotten what turned out to be an unfair advantage. He hadn't asked for the hints from across the room, but he'd put them to use. "Fine," he said through gritted teeth. "Then let's chop the pot and forget the last hand even happened."

"That ain't good enough."

"Chopping the pot means we get our money back. What the hell else do you want from me?"

"How about some blood and a few teeth?"

If George hadn't been such a talker, he might have snuck in the first punch. As it was, he gave Clint more than enough warning before he took a swing at his jaw.

Clint saw the punch coming and almost got out of its way. At the last second, he clenched his muscles and forced himself to take it on the chin. Even though he rolled with the punch a bit, he could still feel its impact rattle his back teeth. Rubbing at his jaw, he asked, "Happy now?"

George looked happy, but in a way similar to a hungry dog that was happy to stumble upon some hapless prey. "Mister, I ain't even started yet."

While Clint was willing to accept a few lumps to pay him back for the little bit of cheating he'd done, he wasn't about to stand there and allow himself to get beaten to a pulp. An asshole like George would surely take full advantage of any situation where he could look like a big man. Fortunately for Clint, this asshole didn't have nearly enough to put Clint down for good.

The second punch was a short uppercut into Clint's stomach. That one landed with a solid thump and was immediately followed by another. Clint turned and brought both arms in close to catch a piece of it. The rest of

George's fist was deflected to bounce against Clint's ribs. Undeterred by that glancing blow, George took a wild swing that was intended to take Clint's head off. Instead, Clint stepped away and to the side so George's fist chopped through empty air. Even better than that, George's momentum caused his arm to sail well past Clint's head, leaving his upper body extended at an awkward angle.

Unable to resist such a prime target, Clint delivered a straight right cross that cracked against George's face and sent him staggering into another card table. When a few of the players at that game were knocked away from their seats, Clint thought the fight would spread like wildfire. Those other gamblers didn't join the brawl, but one of them did hand George a half-empty bottle.

"You wanna take the side of some cheatin' darkie?" George snarled. "Then you'll get beat like one!" When George tried to swing his bottle at Clint, he was stopped before his arm could move halfway through the motion.

The black man who'd been sitting at the faro table had stepped forward to grab George's arm. "You aren't gonna beat anyone, George," he said. "And I already told you before, nobody cheated you when you were at my table."

"Bullshit."

Now that George's momentum had been broken, Clint was able to walk right up and grab the bottle from his hand. Rather than use it as any sort of weapon, he placed it upon another table. "You threw your tantrum," Clint said. "Now let's either get back to our game or part ways like men."

"I'll part your damn scalp like a man," George said.

Clint stood his ground as if he didn't have a care in the world. In fact, he used every sense he had to take in his surroundings. As far as he could tell, everyone who was close enough to do anything was standing back to enjoy the show.

At first, Clint thought that George had actually come to his senses. Then, the red-faced gambler snapped his hand down toward the gun at his hip. Clint's gun hand moved in a quick, fluid motion that pulled his modified Colt from its holster and pointed it at George. The move had been so fast that George reacted as if he'd just witnessed a miracle. His eyes grew even wider when the barkeep stomped forward with a sawed-off shotgun in his hands.

"You boys don't put those guns away, I'll be forced to use mine," the barkeep said. After Clint holstered his Colt, the barkeep added, "All the same, you men had better leave."

A flicker of fear drifted across George's face as he pondered what could happen once both he and Clint were outside. Rather than let it grow into anything more, Clint raised his hands and said, "I'll be on my way. I'm sure George would like to finish his game."

FOUR

Clint walked away from Pace's, knowing several sets of eyes were watching him go. He turned the first corner he could, just so his back wasn't facing those particular windows. Even after he'd gone halfway down the next street, he knew he was being followed.

It started as a bristling at the back of his neck. It was a cool night, but not enough to create the chill he felt making its way along his spine. After spending so many years being ambushed, tracked, and hunted by all manner of dangerous men, he knew that chill all too well. The footsteps he heard upon the boardwalk behind him only sealed the deal.

Passing a narrow alley so the next one was a fair distance from him, Clint stopped and turned around. Compared to what he'd been expecting, the person following him was a very pleasant surprise.

"Oh," the tall faro dealer said. "You startled me."

Clint took in the sight of her with a quick up-and-down glance. She looked a bit taller from this distance, but also looked a whole lot prettier. Her long black hair had been hastily tied back, and several strands were loose and in her face as the wind blew. She'd wrapped a light shawl around herself to keep her shoulders warm, but wasn't holding it tightly enough to keep him from getting a good look at the generous amount of cleavage displayed by her low-cut dress. In the dim light of the moon and of the torches lining the street, her skin looked smooth and damn near flawless.

"I'm really sorry about all of that," she said.

"Why?" Clint asked. "Did you make George into such a loud-mouthed asshole?"

She laughed in a way that allowed a beautiful smile to cross her face. "No, but I did put you in an awkward position. I don't know how many times I've told that man to keep his cards covered, but he never takes my advice."

"Let me guess. He said he didn't want no advice from a woman."

"Actually, he kept trying to get me into bed. Every time I spoke a word to him, he took it as an invitation for him to get under my skirts."

Clint shook his head and chuckled. "That one's a real piece of work."

"Yes, but we did sort of cheat him."

"I know. That's why I gave back the money I won from the last couple of hands."

She blinked and cocked her head in disbelief. "You did?"

"Yep. On my way out."

"Let me guess. He told you to go to hell."

"No," Clint replied. "He tried to get twice as much out of me as I won during that whole game."

"He is a piece of work."

Both of them walked down the street. Since he could tell there wasn't anyone else lurking about or dogging their trail, Clint allowed himself to relax. "So, your name's Delilah?"

"How'd you know?"

"Surely you don't think a woman who looks like you could deal faro around so many men without being noticed."

"I thought most of their interest ended once they stared at me for a few hours," she replied.

"The men at my table knew more than that. Still," he added, "we all did tend to watch you awfully close when we had the chance."

Smiling again, she told him, "That's all right. Men tend to spend more time at my table when they've got a nice view. Also, I kind of enjoy it when some men like what they see."

The glint in her eye and the way she moved a bit closer to Clint made it clear that she wasn't referring to any of the locals. Continuing along without acknowledging the way she brushed against him, Clint asked, "Who's that man working your table with you?"

"That'd be Carl. He keeps track of the cash and counts down the hands that are dealt. George doesn't have much good to say about him either."

"He says Carl cheated him."

"George says that about everyone," Delilah pointed out. "He only gets it right some of the times. In Carl's case, he's dead wrong. I don't need the headaches that come along with having a cheat working at my table. The odds in faro are stacked in my favor well enough without that."

"George was ready to tear his head off," Clint said. "There has to be something behind that."

Delilah shrugged and clasped her hands behind her back. That way, she could stroll beside Clint while also arching her back just enough for her chest to swell a bit more beneath her shawl. "Carl has to keep his head down in that place just because of his color. Most folks hardly seem to take notice of him since he's so quiet, but men like George will take a swing at anyone he thinks won't swing back."

Clint didn't have any reason to doubt that. The wild look in George's eyes was more than enough to back up her explanation. "I'd hate to think our little indiscretion would bring any harm to an innocent man. Do you think Carl might need someone watching his back?"

"When I left, George was sitting in his chair, bragging about how he ran you out of there. Carl was in his seat and all was right with the world." She glanced over at him and took a few minutes to study Clint in much the same way that he'd studied her earlier. "You could've kept George's money, you know. God only knows how many poor souls he's cheated over the years."

"Is that why you helped me with all those nods and scowls?"

"He tried fixing my game a few times. Every time I caught him, he threw a bigger fit. Guess I saw the chance for some comeuppance and I took it."

"Next time, just be sure your accomplice knows what's going on," Clint told her.

Suddenly, Delilah stepped in front of him and stopped Clint by placing a hand flat upon his chest. Staring directly into his eyes, she slowly moved her hand down along his stomach. "If you've got a warm bed nearby, I'd like to make it up to you."

"There now," Clint replied with a grin. "All you had to do was ask."

FIVE

While Clint and Delilah made it back to the room he was renting, they didn't quite make it to the bed. As soon as he'd let her in, she began peeling away her clothes, one layer at a time. Her shawl was the first to go, followed by her dress and the slips under her skirts. That left her wearing a black corset, black lacy panties, and boots that were laced up to just above her knees. Delilah turned on the balls of her feet and stopped Clint once more with a well-placed hand.

"You were watching me the whole time you were in Pace's," she said.

Clint shrugged. "Not the whole time. I did need to glance at my cards every now and then."

She shook her head while slipping her fingers between the buttons of his shirt. "You were watching me. How else would you see my signals?"

"Those weren't hard to miss."

"Really? What about this one?" With that, she pulled her hand back and tore his shirt open. One of Clint's buttons even popped loose and skittered across the floor.

Taking hold of her hips and pulling her close, Clint said, "I believe I understood that signal just fine." He then placed his lips upon her mouth and kissed her. It started off well enough, but the kiss gathered more heat with every second that passed. Before long, Delilah reached up to run her fingers through his hair while opening her lips to ease her tongue into his mouth.

Clint could feel the warmth from her body as if he were standing next to an open flame. He eased his hands along her sides, tracing a line up to her shoulder blades and then back down to the trim curve of her firm backside. Delilah purred in the back of her throat as she felt his hands caress her. Clint could even feel her smile as she continued to kiss him.

Without saying a word, she moved him back. All she needed to do was take a step forward to get Clint to take a step back. When he felt the backs of his legs knock against a chair, he dropped down onto the seat rather than kick it out of his way.

Delilah tugged at the buckle of his gun belt, but Clint was the one to remove it and set it down. All the while, she busied herself by getting his jeans down, and then knelt on the floor between his legs. In a matter of seconds, Clint felt her lips close around the tip of his cock.

"Jesus." He sighed as she took every inch of him into her mouth. Clint placed his hands on the back of her head and had just enough time to catch his breath before her tongue went to work.

As she lowered her head, she slid her tongue forward to lick the bottom of his shaft. Then, as she eased up again, she flicked her tongue to tease him every inch of the way. Clint could only handle a small bit of that before he pulled her head up and away from him.

"You didn't like that?" she asked, knowing perfectly well how much he'd liked it.

Rather than play along with her question, Clint motioned for her to stand up, and then slid her panties off. Pulling her toward him, he felt her hips wriggle as she spread her legs and climbed onto his lap. Delilah looked down at him and placed her hands upon his shoulders while Clint reached down to position his rigid cock between her thighs. The moment she felt it slip between the moist lips of her pussy, she lowered her self onto it.

She let out a long sigh as Clint's erection drove deeper into her. When she finally reached its base, she slowly shifted her hips until he was hitting the right spot inside of her. "Oh my," she said. "That's—"

Gripping her hips a little tighter, Clint pushed himself up into her a little more. It was just enough of a surprise to snap Delilah's eyes wide open and tighten her grip on his shoulders.

"Oh *my*," she groaned.

She leaned forward and wrapped her arms around Clint's neck. Resting her head against his, Delilah rocked back and forth in time to Clint's rhythm. The chair creaked beneath them, but it wasn't supporting both of their weight. Delilah's legs were long enough for her to keep her body at the proper height and angle for Clint to slide easily in and out of her.

Just when he hit his stride, Clint felt her speed up. She cinched her arms around him a bit tighter and ground her hips in little circles every now and then. Soon, she was moaning softly in his ear and riding his cock until she climaxed. Before he could follow suit, Clint lost his grip on her completely.

"Where are you going?" he asked as she stood up and backed away from the chair. Clint was about to get up and chase her when Delilah stopped, turned around, and then climbed onto his lap again.

This time, she wasn't facing him. Clint admired the smooth line of her back after she unlaced her corset and pulled it off. Now that she was naked except for her boots, she arched her back and tousled her hair as if to fully enjoy the feeling of cool air on her bare skin. Delilah's long, wavy hair flowed all the way down to the uppermost curve of her buttocks. There was a pair of dimples there that brought an admiring grin to Clint's face.

Delilah leaned forward to take hold of his cock and guide it into her. Once it was inside, she leaned forward again, placed her hands upon Clint's knees, and started riding him. From his angle, Clint could only see the motion of Delilah's hair as she tossed it about. When he looked down, he could see her tight little ass bouncing in his lap. He placed his hands upon her hips to guide her, but that was like trying to steer a wild bronco with nothing but a thin set of reins. He could somewhat adjust her movements, but he sure as hell couldn't slow her down. Then again, she was doing just fine on her own.

Clint leaned back and let her go. Pretty soon, she leaned back a little as well, which allowed him to reach around and cup her breasts with both hands. Delilah pressed her hands on top of his and bounced straight up and down. Clint could feel her nipples becoming harder against his palms. When he felt a tide rising up within him, he grabbed her hips and held her tightly.

This time, she wasn't able to resist him. Delilah wriggled her hips some more, practically begging him to pump into her. Clint obliged with a series of straight trusts between her legs. She even stood up a bit to give him some room to thrust into her even harder.

When he felt his climax approaching, Clint pulled her down and drove all the way up into her. Both of them moaned loudly as he released inside of her. Delilah stood up, turned around, and then sat in his lap facing him. Rather than take him inside again, she rubbed her wet pussy against his cock and smiled hungrily.

"I've been wanting to do that all night long," she said.

"Is that what all those grins were about?"

"That, and wanting you to take George for every cent he had."

"Sorry to disappoint you," Clint said as he got up and stretched his legs.

Delilah stood as well and pressed herself against his chest, wrapping her arms around him. When she lifted a leg to rub against Clint's thigh, he thought she might entangle him so he couldn't move. "Believe me," she told him, "the last thing you did was disappoint."

"You think I'll be able to enter that poker tournament?"

"Why don't you rest up and I'll make you forget there's anything else outside of this room?"

It wasn't exactly the cash prize he'd been after, but Clint felt awfully lucky to hear those words.

SIX

Clint went to bed at a decent time, but didn't actually get any sleep until the wee hours of the morning. Since he didn't have anything in particular to do that day, he stretched out and let Delilah apologize a few more times for getting him kicked out of Pace's. Since he'd played his own part in that debacle, Clint did a few favors for her in return. By the time she left his room, he could barely walk straight.

After throwing on some clothes, he went to the hotel's dining room and cleaned up the odds and ends left over from the regular breakfast service. He washed it down with some warm coffee and stepped outside for some fresh air. It was a brisk morning and the bright, cloudless sky did nothing to take away the chill. Even so, the breeze felt good on Clint's face and he took a moment to savor it.

The hotel was situated near a busy corner. As Clint looked in the direction of the stable where he'd left Eclipse, he thought it might be time to get moving. After all, he'd stayed in Trickle Creek for a lot longer than he'd expected, and Eclipse had surely gotten his fill of greens by now. If not, the Darley Arabian would have to toughen up and remember who carried the reins in that relationship. Clint smirked at the thought of having to teach Eclipse a lesson.

Sometimes he thought that horse was smart enough to teach *him* a thing or two.

Clint must have still been smiling when he looked across the street, because the man watching him from there smiled right back at him. Carl's grin only lasted a second or two before he lowered his head so the wide brim of his hat covered a good portion of his face. The black man was close to Clint's height, but carried himself in a way that made him seem shorter. He crossed the street in quick steps and stopped just outside of Clint's reach.

"Begging your pardon, sir," Carl said. "I don't know if you know me, but I'm—"

"The fellow from Pace's Emporium," Clint said in a friendly tone. "Name's Carl, isn't it?"

Carl lifted his head again and almost straightened up to his full height. "Yes, it is. Carl Malloy. And you'd be Clint Adams?"

"That's right. I'd like to thank you for stepping in on my behalf with George." Clint extended a hand to the other man and left it out there when it wasn't shaken. Taking a step toward Carl, he added, "Sorry if there was more trouble after I left. When things got stirred up, I had no idea George would pull you into it."

Carl took Clint's hand and shook it. He had a strong grip, but was obviously holding back. "There wasn't any more trouble. Leastways, no more than usual. George got back to his game and lost all that money you handed over."

"I kind of figured that's how it would go. Knowing for certain makes it a lot easier to bear." After a few seconds of awkward silence, Clint tipped his hat and started to walk away. "If that's it, I suppose I'll be moving along."

"Where are you headed?"

"To the stable. Any more rest and my horse will start to expect such easy living whenever his legs get tired."

Practically jumping to catch up with Clint, Carl fell into step beside him and asked, "You're not leaving, are you?"

"I'm not about to buy a house and sink roots here."

"I . . . have a proposition for you."

Clint stopped. "What kind of proposition?"

After gulping down a few deep breaths, Carl spoke in a rush. "I want to hire you."

"Hire me for what?"

"I heard a few things about you, Mister Adams. After what happened yesterday, you can see for yourself what kind of trouble sprouts up around me. Most of that trouble comes from men like George."

Not liking where the conversation was headed, Clint narrowed his eyes and hooked his thumbs over his gun belt. "Yeah?"

"Well, from what I've heard . . . folks call you the Gunsmith."

"They do."

Carl shifted on his feet, straining to get out the words he wanted to say. "They must call you that for a reason."

"I can do some fine work with firearms, but my wagon with all my tools isn't around. Do you have some weapons that need repairing?"

"No. I heard that you know how to use a gun every bit as well as you know how to fix 'em."

Nodding, Clint said, "Finally you arrive at it. You want to hire me as a gunman?"

"Yes, but—"

"I'm not a professional killer," Clint interrupted. "Anyone who told you that was wrong. There's no way for you to know any better, so I'll chalk this up to a simple mistake. Now, if you'll excuse me, I've got things to do."

There was more Carl wanted to say, but Clint was in no mood to hear it. Stories about the Gunsmith had spread far and wide for quite some time. Clint was no stranger to that. Sometimes, those stories worked in his favor when someone in a saloon wanted to buy him a beer for a job well done or bend his ear over a game of cards. Sometimes, those stories proved to be a pain in Clint's ass when they got other men worked up enough to take a shot at him for no good reason. Every now and then, a young would-be killer would try to make a name for himself by being the man to kill the Gunsmith. Clint didn't lump Carl into that category, but he also didn't appreciate being treated as a killer for hire.

"Mister Adams?" Carl squeaked.

Turning around, Clint saw a genuinely apologetic look on the other man's face. He reminded himself that Carl was simply working on some bad information, then asked, "Yeah?"

"I . . . I mean . . . sorry about that. About the misunderstanding and all."

"No harm done. You have a good day."

"Yeah. I suppose I'll try."

SEVEN

Clint spent a little time in the stable with Eclipse. Although the fee he'd paid for the Darley Arabian to stay there had included feed, it obviously hadn't included much in the way of brushing. Since the liveryman had made himself scarce after getting paid, Clint ran a brush through Eclipse's mane and then walked toward his saddlebags. The moment Clint reached for the saddle, Eclipse began to fret.

"None of that, boy," Clint said. "You're lucky you got the rest and greens you were after. If you start getting fussier, I may have to start looking for a new horse."

Going by the way Eclipse stomped and shook his head, it was hard to be certain he didn't understand everything Clint was saying.

"Oh, for Christ's sake." Clint grunted as he dropped the saddle and hunkered down next to the stallion's front hooves. "What's the matter with you?"

"Do you always talk to your horse so much?"

Clint had heard someone walking toward his stall, so he wasn't taken by surprise. He hadn't expected to hear Delilah's voice, however. Just to be sure, he looked up to see who'd spoken. It was Delilah, all right. She wasn't wearing the fancy clothes from the night before, but that didn't hamper her looks any. In fact, the simple brown skirt and white blouse were downright attractive. Then again, knowing what was under those garments allowed Clint to be attracted to her without stretching his imagination very far.

"Sure, I talk to my horse," he replied. "Don't you?"

"I don't own a horse."

"Then you shouldn't be so quick to judge."

Delilah stepped close enough to reach out and pat the white spot on Eclipse's nose. Almost immediately, the stallion calmed down. "Do you think he understands what you say?"

Gripping a hoof under one arm, Clint looked up and said, "Of course. Otherwise, I'd be crazy to flap my gums so much."

She chuckled and continued to rub Eclipse's muzzle. "He's a fine looking creature. Is something wrong with his foot?"

Clint let the hoof drop and went around to grab hold of the other front leg. Eclipse allowed him to grip his hoof without putting up too much of a struggle. "He's been awfully fidgety. I thought he was just tired after too many long rides, but I'm thinking it may be something else. Aw, come on!"

Huffing and grunting, Eclipse shifted his weight and pulled his leg free from Clint's grasp. When Clint tried to get hold of it again, Eclipse bobbed his head and protested loudly.

"Ease up!" Clint barked.

Grudgingly, Eclipse stayed still long enough for Clint to continue his examination.

"He didn't like that very much." Delilah cooed. "Did you, boy?"

"No, he didn't," Clint said through gritted teeth. "I'm thinking I may have been wrong right from the start. If there's something I missed, I'll feel awfully foolish for putting him up in a stable and paying extra for greens."

"What could be wrong with him?" Delilah asked. "Is he sick?"

"Nah. The way he's fretting, it strikes me more as something like a cracked shoe or maybe a pebble jammed up in the wrong place." After struggling a bit more, Clint let go of Eclipse's hoof and let out a tired breath. "Nothing here, though."

After losing interest in Eclipse, Delilah asked, "You got a moment?"

Clint was crouched near Eclipse's left flank, doing his best to keep from getting knocked over by the fidgeting stallion. He looked up at Delilah and replied, "Sure, I'm not busy here or anything."

"Really?"

"No," he snapped as he grabbed hold of Eclipse's rear leg so he could examine that shoe. "What is it?"

Sighing at having to play second fiddle to a fussy horse, she said, "You can come back and play in the tournament, if you like."

"Is that so?"

"Sure. You didn't really lose, you know."

"Normally, when you get escorted away from a game at the wrong end of a shotgun, that means you're through playing."

She shrugged and scraped at the swinging door that closed Eclipse's stall away from the rest of the stable. "This isn't the first time George has done something like this. Also, someone may have put in a good word for you with the management."

"Someone, huh?"

"Could have been me," she added with a wry grin. "After last night, I'm not so eager for you to leave."

"What about the accusation of cheating?" Clint asked as he took hold of Eclipse's back leg and poked around the edges of that shoe. "Something like that doesn't usually set too well in a tournament."

"The rest of the men at your table spoke up on your behalf," Delilah said. "Jack has played in every tournament Pace's has hosted, and he's butted heads with George more than once." Placing her hands upon her hips, Delilah locked eyes with Clint and stopped just short of stomping her foot. "Are you going to stay or not? I won't beg."

"Really? That may be kind of interesting."

Her expression softened and she tilted her head a bit. "You think so? Perhaps you'd like to see me begging on all fours?"

"That'd definitely be interesting."

"Then stay and see the tournament through."

Just then, Clint furrowed his brow. "Wait a second. Why are you so intent on getting me to stay?"

Once again picking at the stall's door, she replied, "I told you already. Last night was better than—"

"Spare me the compliments," Clint cut in. "There's more to it than that."

She chewed on her lip, perhaps to make herself look more appealing. Her efforts were having an effect on him, but Clint wasn't about to let her know as much. Delilah smiled at him, licked her lips, and then rolled her eyes. She must have thought she wasn't making a dent in his resolve because she dropped her act like a hot rock.

"You must really think a lot of yourself if you expect me to grovel just to keep you in town," she snapped.

Clint got back to examining Eclipse's shoe and laughed under his breath. "I didn't even expect you to come this far to track me down."

"So you think I'm dogging your trail just because you showed me a good time?"

"Isn't that what you just told me?"

Letting out a sigh, Delilah said, "I think you can win that tournament."

"Now you believe in my card-playing skills? That's touching."

"I also . . . may have . . . put some money down on that."

"You bet on me to win the tournament?" Clint asked.

"Maybe just a little." Seeing the look on his face, she added, "Maybe a lot."

"How much?"

"A couple thousand."

Clint let Eclipse's hoof slip from his hands as he jumped to his feet. "A couple thousand? Are you kidding me?"

Now Delilah's wounded innocent act came back in force. She clasped her hands in front of her, tilted her head, and batted her eyelashes as she stepped forward. To put icing on the cake, she even reached out to brush her hands against Clint's chest when she told him, "I know you can do it, Clint. Honestly."

"Was this before or after George started getting sloppy with his cards?"

"Before."

"So that's why you started helping me?" Clint asked.

She shook her head and showed him a smile that was just as naughty as it was nice. "Everything I told you before was true. I just thought we could make a good team."

"So you just had a few thousand dollars lying around to bet on a stranger who could read your signals, huh?" Clint grunted. "That's very fortunate."

"It's not cash. It's money owed to me by some of the regulars at my table. I wagered their markers on you, double or nothing."

"What if I do stay and win?" Clint asked. "Do I get a cut of your wager?"

"Of course." The longer she had to wait for her answer, the more her smile faded. Finally, she asked, "Well? What do you think?"

"I think I found the reason Eclipse was being so fussy."

EIGHT

Since the liveryman was nowhere to be found, Clint searched for what he needed in the immediate area. He found the tools necessary for removing Eclipse's shoe in the far corner of an empty stall. It took a bit of work for Clint to get the shoe off, but once Eclipse knew what was going on he wasn't about to resist. When Clint finally got the shoe off and pried something from the Darley Arabian's hoof, he thought he heard Eclipse sigh with relief.

All this time, Delilah had stayed nearby. She offered to lend Clint a hand every now and then, but he got the impression that she was only making certain he wasn't about to leave. As Clint examined what he'd just pried loose, she got up from her stool and walked closer. "What is that?" she asked.

Holding up a small pair of tongs, Clint studied a thin wedge of metal that was rusted on one side and shiny on the other. "Could be damn near anything," he told her. "Piece of a railroad tie. Chunk of a busted wheel rim. Maybe even shrapnel from an old cannon."

"Really?" Delilah asked as her eyes widened and she leaned in for a closer look. "How interesting! You rode through a battle on your way here?"

"No, I didn't ride through a battle," Clint scoffed as he pitched the metal out a nearby window so it wouldn't get underfoot of any of the horses within the stable. "It's like I said the first time. Could be anything. The important thing is that it's no longer stuck under Eclipse's shoe."

Shifting her focus from the tongs to the man that held them, Delilah asked, "So does this mean you're staying?"

Clint got up and straightened his back. He patted the stallion's side, which caused Eclipse to turn and look at him. The Darley Arabian was tired after all that restlessness, but now just looked relieved. Removing the metal sliver had allowed him to relax the muscles he'd been tensing ever since the sliver had first gotten wedged into his hoof in the first place.

"He's a tough fella," Clint said. "It won't be long before he's ready to run some more."

"But . . . not tonight?" Delilah asked hopefully.

"No. Not tonight."

She giggled, clapped her hands, and even hopped up and down a few times. When she was through with that, she looked just as relieved as Eclipse. "After the way I curled your toes last night, I didn't imagine it would take so long to convince you to spend another night or two with me."

Clint thought about trying to keep a straight face, but decided against it. "You don't need to do any convincing to get me to spend any night with you. I just wanted to know everything going on inside that pretty little head of yours."

"Trust me," she said with a glint in her eye, "you'll never know everything going on inside my pretty little head."

"Fair enough. When does the tournament start?"

"In a few hours. I've already spoken to the owner, and he doesn't mind you playing at Pace's, so long as you don't start any more trouble. Between you and me, though, he knows George is to blame for what happened before. He'll still give you the evil eye when you show up, so nobody else thinks about stepping out of line."

"You already spoke to the management, huh?" Clint asked.

She turned and hurried out of the stable. "I was just being prepared, Clint. See you there!"

Before he could scold her any more, she was gone. Then again, Clint already knew that scolding Delilah wouldn't have done any good anyhow. They'd only known each other for a day or so, which was more than enough for him to tell that she was the kind who was used to having men wrapped around her little finger. When he thought back to the night they'd spent together, Clint figured being wrapped around her wasn't such a bad thing.

"So you'll be stayin' on for a spell?"

Clint didn't see the liveryman, but recognized his voice well enough. Glancing around, he spotted the filthy, potbellied man wandering in through a side door. "Yeah. Looks that way."

"I'll need the fee in advance."

"You don't think I'm good for it?"

Judging by the expression on the stableman's face, the notion of delaying payment was something completely unknown to him. Before smoke came out of his ears, he grunted, "I need it in advance. More, if you want them same greens."

Clint walked over to the stableman while digging some money out of his pocket. As he counted out the proper sum, he asked, "Who around here could tend to my horse?"

"My place ain't good enough for ya?"

"No. I mean someone who could help me nail a shoe back on," Clint said. "Maybe help tend to a bit of a wound."

"Yer horse in a painful way? Maybe it'd be best to put him down and move on. I know where you can pick up a real dandy fer a good price."

Glaring at the stableman, Clint growled, "It's nothing that bad. He just needs a new shoe and a bit of tending to one hoof."

"Oh, is that what you were doin'?" The stableman shrugged and said, "The town doc sees to horses and people alike. He don't work on no shoes, though. I could arrange that for ya."

"I'd appreciate it."

"Ain't free, though."

Clint made sure the stableman saw the money in his hand, but didn't hand any over. "How long will it take to get done?"

"Few days," the stableman said with another shrug.

"How long?"

Staring at the money the way a hungry dog might drool over a steak, the stableman said, "I can probably get it done tomorrow, but it might take until the day after that. I don't know how busy Uncle Tim is."

Clint added a few dollars to the stable fees and handed the money over. "The sooner it gets done, the more appreciative I'll be when I leave."

Despite his dull eyes and slack jaw, the stableman had no trouble interpreting that.

NINE

The tournament was a simple affair. Each man bought in for a certain amount of chips, and losing all your chips meant it was the end of that man's chance to win. With a buy-in at only seventy-five dollars, it was also one of the cheapest tournaments Clint had ever entered. That relatively low fee, however, meant a lot more people could throw their hats into the ring. By the time the first hand was dealt, Clint figured the grand prize had grown to a fairly respectable size.

Just as Delilah had predicted, Clint was given a stern warning the moment he plunked down his entry fee. "Don't expect this back if you force me to kick you out of here again," the barkeep said. He was the same barkeep who'd wielded the sawed-off shotgun when George had thrown his fit yesterday. Judging by the look in his eyes, he was awfully close to reaching for that shotgun again.

"I didn't start it the first time and I won't start anything this time," Clint said. "Did you give this same speech to George?"

"No." Nodding toward the back of the saloon, the barkeep said, "He did."

Clint looked in that direction to find a man who seemed

big enough to hold up that portion of the building on his wide shoulders. A long mustache sprouted from his upper lip like black wax dripping off his face. His crossed arms had the thickness of entwined logs. Even with those natural assets, the big man wore a double-rig holster around his waist.

Perhaps recognizing the surprised expression on Clint's face, the barkeep said, "Les had the day off when you were tossed out."

"Seems that was my lucky day after all."

"You got that right. You'll be playing at that table over there."

Looking to the spot where the barkeep was pointing, he spotted a table with two empty seats. Suddenly, he saw Les straighten up to become even taller. The reason for that made itself known a second later.

"What the hell is this?" George grunted as he and two other men stomped into Pace's Emporium.

"Stay right there, George," the barkeep said. Jabbing a finger at Clint, he said, "You. Get to your table and stay put."

Clint held up his hands and walked away. Les watched him like a hawk until he got to his chair. Then, the big man shifted his gaze to George and watched him with just as much intensity.

Just as his backside was touching his seat, Clint was greeted by a familiar face.

"Hello again, Mister Adams," Wendell said.

Not only was the skinny banker sitting in at another of Clint's games, but he was in the same spot to his right that he'd been at the last game. "I just can't seem to shake you," Clint said. Before Wendell could get the wrong idea, Clint grinned and slapped the skinny man on the back. "Good luck to you."

"Better than our last game, at least," Wendell replied.

The first hands were to be dealt promptly at eight

o'clock, which gave the men in attendance another couple of hours before the tournament got underway. That didn't stop any of the tables from starting games of their own using money from their own pockets. Indeed, those side games were exactly why so many entrants had shown up so early. More often than not, the winners at those private games made out better than the winner of the tournament. Sizing up the others at his table, Clint doubted he'd get quite so lucky.

Next to Wendell was an Irishman named Mack, who wore a dark blue suit and played the part of a professional card sharp. Mack either played the role better than he lived it or he was lying low, because his poker skills weren't overly impressive.

Sitting between Mack and Clint was a kid who had to be in his very early twenties. Just looking at his clothes, anyone might have mistaken him for a cowboy who'd wandered into Pace's for a stiff drink and the company of a pretty girl. He was a nice enough fellow, but seemed even younger the moment he opened his mouth.

"Holee smokes!" the cowboy exclaimed as he raked in a pot that sheer luck had given him. "I sure do like this game."

There was always a chance that the act was something being put on to make the cowboy seem like less of a threat, but Clint doubted that was the case. There simply wasn't an easy way to fake such wide-eyed enthusiasm. If the cowboy wasn't much of a gambler, he at least had some good jokes to help while away the time before the tournament began.

More than once during those hands, the pot was built up well beyond what it might get to in the tournament's early stages. While Mack pulled in enough to make it worth his while to get up and leave before the tournament even started, Clint pulled in enough to make up his entry fee. From then on, it would be just a good night of poker. Of course, he would be dashing some high hopes if he took the night so lightly.

Delilah was at her faro table, doing her best to smile at her players while dealing her cards. All the while, she watched Clint carefully. He guessed she was also getting occasional reports about his progress, because her mood directly reflected his winning and losing streaks, despite the fact that they were nowhere near each other. Considering the circumstances of the way they'd met, Clint tried not to look at her too often.

About a quarter to eight, the fifth player at Clint's table took his seat between Clint and the young cowboy. Bull wore the same clothes as he had the night before, and had the same bland expression on his face.

"Evenin'," Bull said to each of the other players. If he recognized Clint or Wendell, he gave no indication.

When Clint dealt the next hand, Bull was taken aback. "Tournament ain't started yet," Bull said.

"Sure," Clint replied. "These are just friendly games."

"Friendly enough to make ol' Mack rich as hell!" the cowboy chuckled.

Bull looked at his cards and immediately folded. He did the same for every hand after that until the owner of Pace's stepped up to announce the start of the tournament.

TEN

At ten o'clock, the owner of Pace's stepped up again. Clint still didn't know the man's name, but he dressed like a dandy, carried himself like a mayor, and talked like a carnival barker. While most of the men drifted toward the bar or outhouses, Clint glanced over to the faro tables. He may have felt a pull in that direction because Delilah was staring at him hard enough to burn holes through his hat.

Pace's Emporium was packed to the rafters. Apparently, the tournament was known far and wide throughout the area and attracted folks from the entire county. Delilah pointed toward one of the side doors and then said something to Carl, who sat in his usual seat beside her. Since he knew he couldn't exactly get away from her, Clint followed Delilah's direction and shoved his way through the crowd toward the side door.

It was a cool night, but not as chilly as the night before. The side door Delilah had indicated was on the opposite side of the building as the outhouses and opened into a small lot containing a few broken-down old sheds. Clint's nose was sharp enough to pick up the scent of smoked meat coming from one shed. He didn't have a chance to look into any of the others before Delilah hurried out to join him.

"So?" she asked eagerly. "How are you doing?"

"Something tells me you already know the answer to that."

The smile on her face was almost bright enough to light up the entire lot. "I heard you were holding your own."

"And then some."

She clapped and hopped up and down in a way that seemed a little strange coming from a woman as tall as her. "I heard that as well! Perfect!"

"Then why call me out here?" Clint asked. "I could use a beer and maybe some food. Just staying inside would have been a better way to spend the couple of minutes they're giving us."

"I may have heard about your wins and losses, but I'd like to hear the whole story from you. What do you think of your competition?"

"The men at my table are all right. I've already played with two of them, and neither of them has surprised me yet. The kid is lucky as hell, but that never lasts. Mack is a professional. He was lying low at the start, but he's pulled off a few tricks that could make him dangerous."

"You think he can beat you?" Delilah asked.

Clint shrugged and replied, "Now that I know what he's capable of, I should be able to handle him."

"Perfect."

"Is that all? I'm still hungry."

Delilah placed her hand flat upon Clint's chest and shoved him toward the smokehouse. "I am too. That's another reason I brought you out here."

"Don't they serve food inside?"

"Maybe I'd like to serve you something. Call it a little inspiration for my very capable partner." With that, Delilah unbuckled Clint's jeans, and pulled them down a bit as she lowered herself onto her knees. Before Clint could say a word, she'd reached between his legs and found his penis.

He'd been caught off guard and the cold air didn't do

him any favors, but Clint felt his erection grow quickly enough. She cupped him in one hand and wrapped her lips around him so her tongue could work its magic. In a matter of seconds, he was hard as a rock and filling Delilah's mouth.

Clint could hear several voices nearby, but they were either coming from within Pace's or from the outhouses on the other side of the building. She hadn't picked a spot completely in the open, but anyone walking down the closest side street would have glimpsed one hell of a show. Perhaps that very thing got Delilah worked up. She sucked on him hungrily, grabbing his hips and working her head back and forth with growing momentum.

When Clint reached down to pull Delilah to her feet, she looked up at him and smiled. "We don't have enough time for that," she whispered. "Just let me do the inspiring."

Clint might have liked to do a few things to her, but he wasn't about to argue with her proposition. Instead, he leaned against the smokehouse and sifted his fingers through Delilah's long black hair as she wrapped her lips around his cock once more.

The closer Clint got to his climax, the more Delilah reacted. She moaned deeply at the back of her throat, sending a powerful hum all the way through Clint's body. He closed his eyes and held her head still as he began pumping in and out of her mouth. She took to that just fine, and pressed her tongue against the base of his cock as he slid in and out. The moment he eased up, she took control again by sliding her wet lips along every inch of his shaft.

One more of her throaty moans was all Clint could take. He exploded in her and she swallowed every last drop before letting him help her to her feet.

"Now that's what I call inspiration," Clint said as he hitched up his jeans and buckled his belt.

She led him inside and ordered them both a drink. Clint had a beer while she tossed back a shot of whiskey. Players were drifting back to their tables, and the owner of the place looked ready to make another one of his grand announcements.

Once some more bodies cleared away, Clint was able to get a better look at Delilah's faro table. "You might want to get back to your game. And you might want to take some muscle with you."

"What?" she asked as she snapped her head in that direction. "Why?"

Clint didn't need to say another word. She was more than able to see George and two other men clustered around Carl. They were too far away for Clint to hear what was being said, but he knew a pack of wild animals when he saw one.

"You want some help?" Clint asked.

Delilah pushed him back as she walked forward. "No. You won't win me any money by getting kicked out of the tournament. Just get back to your game and let me handle this."

While he wasn't comfortable with letting a woman walk into a potentially bad spot, Clint felt a lot better when he saw Les moving to meet her at the table. When she got there, she gave George and the other two a piece of her mind, swatting at the men and shoving through them as she did. One of George's friends looked ready to start something, but thought better of it when Les's massive hand slapped against his shoulder.

Clint smirked as he watched the troublemakers try to maintain their dignity while putting some distance between themselves and Les. The hulking guard didn't even need to make a move toward his guns to put the fear of God into those three. Clint couldn't help but notice the looks that were being tossed toward Carl, however. Obviously there was some unfinished business between George and the quiet black man.

During the entire spat, from the time when George had been spouting off to when Les came to break up the small group, Carl hadn't lifted a finger. He'd stayed perched upon his stool, kept his head down and didn't make one threatening move. Some men, however, wouldn't look at that kind of behavior as peaceful. They'd see it as weakness, and if a wild animal sensed weakness, it would only be a matter of time before they attacked again.

"Back to your tables, gentlemen," the dandy saloon owner announced. Deferring to a few of the other players, he added, "And ladies."

George wandered back to his chair and Clint did the same. Carl's predicament was over for the time being, which meant it was time to play some cards.

ELEVEN

It seemed highly doubtful that any high-caliber professional gamblers even knew where Trickle Creek was. That, combined with the relatively small stakes of the tournament, meant the games played that night wouldn't exactly grow to epic proportions. Throughout the next several hours, Clint found himself relaxing into an easy pace with the men at his table.

Every so often one of those men would surprise him, but they mostly lived up to the expectations Clint had formed after first making their acquaintance. The cowboy was good for a laugh, but was on his way to being broke. Wendell and Bull played just as they had the night before, while Mack provided some real competition. All in all, it made for a fun evening. By around two in the morning, Clint sat behind a healthy stack of chips and was on a first-name basis with everyone in the saloon responsible for serving drinks.

"Hey, Sandy," Clint hollered as he leaned back in his chair and waved to a stout woman carrying a tray. "Another round for my friends."

"Friends, hell," Mack said. "I'll keep taking your money no matter how many drinks you buy."

"Wouldn't have it any other way."

The drinks came and the next hand was dealt moments before the owner announced that it would be the last of both for the day. The cowboy was the first to act and when he looked at his cards, he winced. It was an obvious tell, but had proven to be an accurate one. "I bet five," the kid said.

Picking up on the tell and too tired to be sly about it, Mack threw in a handful of chips. "Another twenty."

Wendell looked at his cards a few times, reached for his chips, checked his cards again, and then called.

Clint checked his hand. When he pushed his chips in, he made sure to glare at the kid and then snap a quick look over to Mack. The first man was already shaky, so intimidating him wasn't hard. The second man didn't quite know whether to attribute Clint's confidence to the cards he'd been dealt or the beer he'd been drinking.

After silently checking his cards, Bull tossed them away. He might not have been much of a risk-taker, but he knew the game and could read the players well enough to come out slightly ahead by the end of the night. He held on to the deck and dealt the next round. The cowboy took three cards, Mack stood pat, Wendell took two, and Clint took one.

"Twenty to me, huh?" the kid asked. "Any of you fellas trying to bluff me?"

Without taking his eyes from Clint, Mack said, "You don't want to call, boy. So don't."

"Yeah, you're right." The cowboy tossed away his cards and stood up. "Do I just leave my chips here?"

"Yeah."

"All right, then."

Mack didn't take any pleasure in shoving the kid out of the game so easily. He simply looked at his cards once, set them down, and then folded his hands over them like a small tomb marking their final resting place. "How much you got left, Adams?"

"Not quite as much as you," Clint replied.

"Have you even looked at that other card you were dealt?"

Tapping the neat stack of cards in front of him, Clint shrugged. "Don't need to."

"You haven't looked at it. If your hand was so good already, you wouldn't have needed another one. So you're waiting for me? Fine. The bet's a hundred."

Where Clint had yet to look at his replacement card, Wendell couldn't stop looking at his. Now that the bet had been made, he looked at them twice as much. Finally, he shook his head and shoved his cards toward Bull. "You two are going to fight this out, so I won't get caught in the middle. It's too late for that kind of nonsense."

"It's never too late for any kind of nonsense," Clint replied. "I raise another fifty."

That caused one of Bull's eyebrows to rise. Although he didn't say much, he clearly enjoyed watching antics like this one at his table.

Mack, on the other hand, wasn't enjoying himself much at all. Every muscle in his face tightened up, and he lifted one finger to rub idly under his nose. Every other second, his eyes darted to the top card on Clint's stack. "You haven't looked at that card. I know it."

Clint knew it too, but merely took another drink of beer and stretched his feet out as if he was content to sit there all night and all day.

"You're a good player, Adams," Mack said, more to himself than to Clint. "You gotta have something to be in this hand, but it can't be better than what I got. You're just trying to make me think too hard about this, aren't you? You think I'm tired or you picked up something along the way to make you think I wouldn't call a raise like this." Suddenly, Mack nodded. "All right, then. What if I raised another sixty?"

"You sure about that?" Clint asked. "That'll put just

about everything you took away from Bull and the kid into the middle of the table."

If Mack had been looking for a flinch from Clint, he didn't get it. "Four of a kind, huh?" he speculated. "Or is it just two pair? Were you fishing for something or do you already have a big hand?" When he still didn't get a reaction from Clint, Mack pushed in fifty dollars' worth of chips and said, "All right, then. I'll just call. I've got a straight to the jack. Can you beat it?"

"Well, let's see about that." Clint turned over the four cards he'd kept to reveal the three, five, nine, and ten of spades.

Mack's face darkened and he scowled at the cards in disbelief. "You called with that? You didn't even look at your other card and you raised? I watched you! You didn't look at your fifth card yet! How could you do something that stupid?"

Casually, Clint flipped over the single card he'd asked for. It was the deuce of spades. "Looks like it was a smart play after all."

While Clint raked in the chips, Mack leaned back and shook his head. "You're either real crazy or real stupid."

"You didn't have me pegged for either, did you?"

"No, sir. I sure didn't."

"That's the beauty of poker," Clint said with a grin. "Don't you just love this game?"

TWELVE

"What in the hell was the meaning of that?" Delilah asked as she stomped after Clint.

He'd left Pace's and had just crossed the street when the tall brunette all but ambushed him. "I gambled," he said in his defense. "That's part of the game, you know."

"Gambling is one thing. That was almost a disaster! You could have lost almost all your money on that last hand! You could have ended your entire tournament!"

Clint locked eyes with her and spoke in a measured tone. "Those things can happen whether I look at my cards or not. Poker's not just about who has the best hand. It's about playing against the other people at the table."

"I know that," she said angrily. "But you don't make a raise without even knowing what the hell you've got."

Sighing, Clint shrugged his shoulders and said, "I admit, I didn't think he'd call that last one. Since he did, that shows me a lot about him and the way he bets. If you want to find out all you can about another player, you've got to get your hands dirty."

"You only won because of blind luck," she snarled.

"That's a big part of poker too. Besides," he added as he pulled her closer and dropped his voice to something just above a whisper, "that last hand drove Mack even crazier than it did you. He's got a good head for odds and percentages. He watches everything and thinks he's got every angle figured. Seeing me play like that against him jammed a nice little burr under his saddle. Seeing me win will eat at him for every second of every hour until the next hand is dealt."

As if to prove his point, Mack left Pace's and headed toward one of the nearby hotels. Even from across the street, Clint and Delilah could hear his boots pounding against the boardwalk as he hissed a stream of obscenities to himself.

"Rather than try to outthink someone who already knows the angles," Clint explained, "it's sometimes better to show them a few angles they'd never considered."

"He sure does look pissed," Delilah said.

"Yep."

"And you did take a bite out of his chip stack."

"He'll recover from that well enough," Clint told her. "Just like I would have recovered if I hadn't gotten that fifth spade."

For the first time since she'd stormed after him, Delilah calmed down. "You were planning for what to do after losing that hand?"

"Of course. Nobody makes any big wins without risking some big losses."

"And that was your way of getting under Mack's skin?"

"Yep. Also," Clint added, "I was getting bored."

All of the grief that had been on her face before returned in full force. There was even some redness and swollen veins in her forehead to go along with it. "Do you know how much this tournament is costing me?"

"Yes. You mentioned that."

"Did I also mention I upped the bet on you? If you get knocked out this soon, I'll be in debt to a lot of people for a long time."

"That's your problem," Clint said. "Next time you want to wager more of your money or credit or whatever, you should ask me first."

"And when I do?"

"I'll advise against it," Clint replied.

She looked as if she was going to explode, but eventually reined it in. "Now you're trying to get under my skin, right?"

"Maybe."

Before she could reply to that, Delilah was cut short by some commotion coming from Pace's Emporium. The front door slammed open and Carl hurried outside. The commotion came from the men that followed him outside.

"Don't you walk out on me!" George snarled. He was flanked by the same two men that had backed him up before, which made him talk louder and strut with more confidence than when he'd been alone. "You hear me, nigger? Stand still when I'm addressing you!"

Carl started to straighten up, but quickly hunkered down again and quickened his steps.

"What does he want with Carl?" Clint asked.

Delilah shook her head. "Nothing that's rightfully coming to him, that's for certain. He had words with Carl a few times during the tournament, but I don't know what was said. All Carl would tell me was that it was a personal matter."

"Do you think they'll try to hurt him?"

"I hope not."

Clint stepped away from her and into the street. "That's not good enough."

THIRTEEN

"Excuse me, Carl," Clint said as he planted his feet and squared his shoulders to all four men. "Mind if I have a word with you?"

Carl glanced in Clint's direction, but stopped when he got a good look at who'd asked the question. A smile started to come across his face, but quickly disappeared. "Now might not be such a good time, Mister Adams."

"Yeah," George said. "Now's not a good time. Keep your nose out of our business."

"What business is that?" Clint asked. "Hounding an un-armed man? I guess it's not enough that he's not carrying a gun, but you've also got to outnumber him three to one. That's some real brave business you're conducting."

George furrowed his brow and gritted his teeth. "I said get out of my sight, so that's what you'd best do."

"I don't take orders from you," Clint said.

Judging by the expression on George's face, he didn't cross paths with too many men who defied him with such ease. "You don't, huh? Then how about following a polite suggestion? Get the fuck out of my sight . . . please."

The other two men with George found that amusing. They liked it even more when Clint said, "All right. Since you said please, I suppose we can part ways. Just be sure to mind your manners."

With that, Clint tipped his hat and walked away. Delilah tried talking to him, but Clint simply took her by the arm and dragged her along.

George and his two followers watched Clint for a bit, but let him go when Carl started walking down the street again. "Hey!" George snapped. "I ain't through with you! Get back here. Hey boy! I told you to get back here."

Carl shoved his hands into the pockets of his jacket and hunched over. In a matter of seconds, George slapped a hand down upon his shoulder and stopped him in his tracks. "You owe me for when you cheated me at that goddamn faro game."

"Nobody cheated you," Carl said.

"I been getting cheated at faro and now I'm getting cheated at poker, so don't try to tell me any different!"

"I can't speak for what's been done at the poker table, but my faro game is fair and square."

"Oh, is it now? What do you think the owner of that place will say when I tell him his nigger bean counter has been cheating a good customer?"

"Wh-... when he finds out you're the customer, he'll know better than to believe that mess of lies."

George reacted to that as if he'd been suddenly rapped on the nose. The two men flanking him bristled like dogs protecting a fresh kill.

"You got something to say to Mister Pace, then you say it to him," Carl said. "Now I've got to be on my way."

"You ain't goin' anywhere," George said as he spun Carl around and then buried his fist into the man's stomach.

Carl doubled over and expelled a gust of air. The biggest of George's companions delivered a quick kick to Carl's face, and the other one pulled a knife from a sheath that hung from his belt. He raised the blade up over his head and would have brought it down again if his progress hadn't been stopped by someone grabbing that wrist in a tight grip.

"Now this isn't at all polite," Clint said as he twisted the man's hand and forced him to drop the knife he'd been holding. Without letting go of that wrist, Clint brought the man's arm up and back before stomping his heel into the guy's shin. Not only did the man howl in pain from the stomp, but he was taken off his balance enough to send him toppling over backward.

As soon as the knife hit the street, Clint kicked it under the boardwalk. Like a dog that had been cut loose, George's second partner lunged at him. Rather than sidestep the charging man, Clint lunged straight at him with an outstretched arm. Not only did he get to the charging man quicker than expected, but Clint hit him with enough force to knock him clean off his feet. The impact sent a painful wave all the way up through his shoulder, but Clint didn't let that dim the fierceness in his eyes.

"This ain't your business, Adams!" George bellowed. "But you're about to force my hand."

"About to force your hand?" Clint replied. "I thought I did that well enough by dropping your two associates here."

George's hand drifted toward his gun. "My boys and I weren't gonna make this a shooting matter."

"And I wasn't going to put a bullet into your back," Clint pointed out. "You push this any farther and you and your men will take more than a few bruises home to remind you what happened tonight."

"Walk away," George warned.

Looking over to Carl, Clint watched the quiet man straighten up and hold his midsection. "What's all this about, anyway?"

George sneered and said, "This one owes me for—"

"I wasn't talking to you!" Clint barked in a voice that rolled down the street and practically cut George off at the knees. Shifting his eyes back to Carl, Clint lowered his voice to a more civil tone and asked, "What's this about, Carl?"

"He wants more chips for the tournament," Carl replied.

"So maybe he should learn to play better poker."

"He wants me to put them on his stack so they're waiting for him when the next round starts. He says he'll forget about talking to Mister Pace if I do that."

Clint nodded slowly and looked over to George. "So, after all this talk about being cheated, you want someone to help you cheat? That would be funny if it wasn't so pathetic."

"Pathetic?" George said. "If I wasn't cheated before, I'd be in better shape now. Leastways, I wouldn't have to scrape and crawl to put together the entry fee."

"If you couldn't afford seventy-five dollars, you shouldn't be in the tournament."

"That's what I said," Carl chimed in.

George vehemently turned on the black man and snarled, "You can't say a damn thing to me, boy! I'll have your help or I'll have your hide."

"You'll shut your damn mouth and go home," Clint said. "Or do I need to kick you and your boys around some more to put you in the right frame of mind?"

The other two men had gotten up and stood facing Clint. They looked ready for a fight, but they weren't about to jump without being told to do so. Even as he backed away, George stabbed his finger at Carl as he said, "I know where to find you, asshole. I won't ask for any help with the tournament, because you'd probably just go squealing to Mister Pace anyhow. But I will have the money back that you cheated from me. I'll have it in cash or I'll make your bitch sister work it off for me the hard way."

Shaking his head, Clint asked, "Are you really too stupid to know when to quit?"

Nodding smugly, George motioned to his two associates and said, "Come on. Let's leave these two lovebirds alone."

The three men put on a tough act for the first few steps. Once they got a little farther away, they were more than happy to rush around a corner and out of Clint's line of fire.

FOURTEEN

Carl walked along the side of the street, shaking his head and muttering, "I really wish you hadn't done that."

Walking beside him, Clint replied, "Would you rather I just stand back and let them kill you?"

"They wouldn't have killed me. Just scared me."

"One of them drew a knife."

Stopping and hunching over, Carl wrapped his arms across his belly as if he was about to vomit.

"What are you carrying?" Clint asked.

"Nothing."

"What is it? Are you carrying something George and those others were after?"

Dropping his voice to a harsh whisper, Carl said, "It's some of the money from the tournament fees. Mister Pace trusts me to take them to the bank because nobody pays me any attention anyhow. He says it's like I'm invisible around here."

Now that he'd spotted the bundle tucked under Carl's jacket, Clint asked, "How much are you carrying?"

"Little more than half of the fees."

"And he doesn't let you carry a gun?"

Carl shook his head. "I tried carrying a gun when I first

came to town. That just stirred up more trouble than it was worth. Mister Pace is right. I am invisible around here. Folks hardly tolerate me, so there's no reason for anyone to assume I'd be trusted with any money."

"Mind if I walk with you to the bank?"

"Guess not."

Clint fell into step with the other man and looked about. The streets were all but empty, and the folks who did see Carl mostly nodded at him. "From what I can tell, people around here like you well enough."

"I suppose."

"Is this what you came to me for earlier?" Clint asked. "To make sure you get that money to the bank?"

"Not as such. I didn't know I'd be doing this until about a half hour ago. It did have to do with what happened, though."

"You mean with George."

Carl nodded. "Him and his kind kick me around because they know nobody around here will do anything to stop him. Folks may wave or smile real kindly at me when they're crossing the street, but nobody's gonna lift a finger against someone like him if he decides to rob me. A man like that George will rob me as long as he knows it's open season. Now he says he's coming after my kin."

"Why would he do that?"

"Why would he do any of it? 'Cause he can get away with it."

Clint would have liked to say that wasn't enough of an explanation. He would have liked to say that a man would need more reason than that to terrorize someone or their family. The simple truth of the matter was that he'd seen a lot worse happen on account of much flimsier excuses. One of George's friends had already tried to stab Carl, so it wasn't much of a stretch to imagine things getting worse.

"Let's drop off that cash," Clint said. "Hopefully George is skulking around somewhere so he'll see you're not carrying anything. Next time, maybe you should carry a gun when you're doing something like this."

"That's just the thing, Mister Adams. That's what I came to you for the last time."

"And I told you before, I'm not a gun for hire."

"I don't want to hire you as a gunman," Carl insisted. "I want you to teach me how to use a gun. From what I hear, you know an awful lot on the subject."

Clint could already see the bank at the end of the street. It was a tall, narrow building with a small front window. The place had either had trouble before or was simply ready for it, because light from one of the torches on the street cast a glimmer upon steel bars behind the glass. "You can save your money. We're almost there."

Carl kept his head down and didn't say anything until they reached the bank. When he got there, he took the bundle of money from his jacket and tapped on the front door. A few seconds later, a little old man scurried from a back room holding a candle in a dented metal holder. He opened the door and snatched the bundle like a rat grabbing a morsel that had been dropped from the dinner table. Without so much as a how-do-you-do, he shut the door and locked it.

"This isn't the job I wanted you to do."

"I know," Clint sighed. "I just don't see what you think I can do for you. There's nothing I can teach you about a gun that'll help with George. At best, you'll get quick enough to draw and accurate enough to kill him. After that, you get strung up for murder."

"A man should be able to defend his family," Carl said.

"Then go home and defend them like any other man. Get a hunting rifle or a shotgun. For a rodent like George, all you'll need to do is fire a shot over his head to send him running. You just need to stand up for yourself and make some noise, not spill blood."

Shaking his head, Carl grumbled, "I can't just make noise. Nobody around here listens. If I stand up to the wrong man, I get locked up. If I make too much of a fuss after that, I get strung up. I need to learn how to handle a gun, Mister Adams, and I need to learn real quick. The only man that can do that is someone like the Gunsmith. I'll pay you for your time or even work out a trade. I got plenty of smithing tools back home. They belonged to my uncle and they're in good enough condition. Any gunsmith would do well to have them."

"I suppose I could use some good tools."

"Really?" Carl asked as he put on a wide, hopeful smile.

"Sure. Let's see what you've got."

FIFTEEN

Carl told him it was a short walk to his house, but Clint wound up covering twice as much ground as he'd anticipated. Delilah only let him out of her sight after making sure to tell him about a dozen times to rest up and prepare for the following day. By the time he finally arrived at the little cabin on the farthest edge of town, Clint was ready to get his rest in the closest convenient pile of straw.

Despite being within a stone's throw of town, Carl's house felt more like a small ranch on its own little piece of property. Only one side of the house faced the town of Trickle Creek, while the rest of it looked out onto open country, a small rise, and a crooked, sorry excuse for a stream that may very well have been the town's namesake. Even at this late hour, someone was at the door to greet the two men before they got close enough to open it for themselves.

The woman was a foot shorter than Clint and had her full, wavy hair tied back by a bandanna. Clint couldn't tell much about her build because she was dressed in a sleeping gown that hugged her figure almost as well as a gunnysack. Her skin wasn't as dark as Carl's, but her eyes and facial features showed the family ties that bound them.

"What took you so long to get here?" she asked as she propped her hands upon her hips. "I was worried sick."

"Ran into a bit of trouble," Carl said.

"Trouble? Are you all right?"

"I walked all the way home, didn't I?"

She scowled at Carl and then turned her attention to Clint. "And who's this?"

"I'm Clint Adams. Pleasure to meet you." As he stepped forward, Clint held out his hand. She shook it reluctantly, which also gave him a chance to get a better look at her face. Even in the dark, he could make out her high cheekbones and full lips. Her eyes may have been angry at the moment, but it was easy to tell they'd be pretty once there wasn't so much fire in them.

"Since my sister isn't of a mind to be neighborly, I'll do the honors," Carl said. "Her name's Sadie and she's pleased to meet you."

"I can say for myself who I'm pleased to meet," she snapped. Shrugging as if she was surprised to hear that come from her own mouth, Sadie nodded to Clint and asked, "Did you help my brother out of his trouble?"

"Yes, ma'am."

She smirked at the formality in Clint's tone and said, "Then I am pleased to meet you."

"Can we come inside now or should we just freeze out here?" Carl asked.

"Come on in. Nobody's stopping you," Sadie replied as she stepped aside so both men could walk through the door.

The cabin was somewhat bigger than Clint had been expecting. There was a large space in the center that consisted of a kitchen and dining area at the back, with a sitting room at the front. On either side of that space was a door leading to what must have been bedrooms. The structure was sound enough, but wasn't quite like anything Clint had seen before. "Did you build this yourself?" he asked.

"I had some help from my uncle and a few cousins, but I had a hand in all of it, more or less."

Sadie chuckled once under her breath and said, "Less rather than more, if I remember correctly."

"Maybe Mister Adams would like some coffee," Carl said as he glared at his sister.

Clint shook his head. "No, thanks. I'll just take a look at those tools."

"You're here to look at tools?" Sadie asked. "At this hour?"

"Will you hush?" Carl scolded.

This time, Sadie wasn't about to fight back. She raised her hands in surrender and walked into one of the side rooms. When she opened the door, Clint got a glimpse of a good-sized bed and a wardrobe. He couldn't see much more than that before she shut herself in for the night.

"This is a nice home you've got," Clint said.

"Thank you. I'd hate to have to pick up and leave this place."

"Why would you have to do something like that?"

Carl lowered his head and retreated into his shell like a turtle, in much the same way he'd been doing since Clint had first met him. He didn't answer the question, but he had to have been thinking along the same lines as Clint. Finally, Carl said, "Tools are in a shed outside. Come see for yourself."

Following the other man back outside, Clint didn't even bother looking for a shed. Instead, he let his eyes wander along the jagged line of the horizon that looked out onto Trickle Creek. The town was dark for the most part, but had a few torches lit along the streets. Some of the windows had flickering lights behind them as well, but the whole area seemed to mostly be asleep.

Stopping at a small shed, Carl dug in his pocket for a key and took his time fitting it into a lock on the narrow door. "So, do you think they'll come?"

"Who?"

Carl looked over to Clint with a crooked scowl on his face. "You know who. And before you waste your breath, don't bother trying to tell me you came all this way at this ungodly hour just to look at a shed full of tools."

"Maybe I did and maybe I didn't," Clint admitted. Judging by the way Carl shook his head, he was having a much easier time believing the former rather than the latter.

SIXTEEN

They arrived less than half an hour later.

Clint spotted the first man approaching from the east side of town, circling around to come at Carl's house from the rear. Knowing there would be others, Clint kept looking until he spotted the second man trying to circle around toward the front of the house. Once he had those two picked out, Clint searched for the third.

"I see him," Carl whispered.

Clint looked at the spot where Carl was pointing, but couldn't see anything other than shadows. "Where?"

"Right there. Just passing those trees now."

Squinting at the trees, Clint was finally able to spot movement that couldn't possibly have been caused by the wind or an animal. Nodding, he said, "One of them looks big enough to be the fellow who pulled the knife on you earlier. That means the other two are probably George and his other friend."

"Who else would it be?"

"Missionaries?"

Carl glanced over and laughed under his breath.

"Right," Clint said. "That'd be too much to hope for. Why don't you get inside and make sure your sister is safe."

"I will not hide in the house to leave you out here."

"If you're so capable of doing this, why did you seek out my help in the first place?" When he didn't get a reply to that, Clint said, "That's what I thought."

"At least let me help."

"The best thing you could do for me is get inside and make sure your sister is safe and away from the windows. After that, light a few lanterns inside."

"Moths to a flame, huh?" Carl asked.

"That's the idea." With that, Clint hunched down and rushed away from the house.

He heard Carl go inside, but he wasn't about to stay put long enough to see if the other man carried out his request. Clint was too busy running from shadow to shadow, bush to bush, and tree to tree in order to get closer to the biggest figure he'd spotted. He went for the big one for two reasons. First of all, he knew the big fellow was fairly slow. Second, it would be more difficult for George and the other one to tell what was going on, since the big man already stuck out like a stump.

As Clint made his way around the big man, he didn't even see the lumbering fellow turn in his direction. Only when Clint was less than ten feet away and accidentally stepped on a branch did the big man stop and take notice. By that time, however, it was too late.

Clint stayed low and rushed at the big man with his arms held open wide. When the big man turned to face him, Clint grabbed the man's gun arm and twisted it to the side. He used his other hand to reach along the big man's belt to feel for the blade that had been there before. Sure enough, the man had collected his knife after the last time Clint had taken it from him. Clint relieved him of the blade once again and pressed it up under the big man's chin.

The big man either didn't feel the sharpened steel against his neck or he was tired of being kicked around, because he stuck his free hand straight out to clamp it around Clint's throat. He squeezed and bared his teeth like an animal going in for the kill.

Clint couldn't draw a breath.

In a few seconds, he wouldn't be able to see. Bright red blobs danced across his field of vision as the big man did his damnedest to choke the life out of him. Rather than try to kick or squirm, Clint pressed the one advantage he already had by jamming the blade up under the big man's chin until blood trickled along the handle.

"What are you doing here?" Clint asked.

"Payin' you and the nigger a visit."

"Couldn't leave well enough alone?"

"You and that cheater made things this way," the big man said. "We just aim to finish 'em."

"All right. Let's see what your friends' intentions are." After saying that, Clint turned toward the cabin and shouted, "Hey, George! Looking for me?"

"That's him!" George said from the distance. "Over there! I see him!"

Although the big man started shouting something back, his voice was washed out by the sudden outbreak of gunfire. If Clint needed any confirmation as to whether George meant to kill him or Carl, he had it now. Simply hearing Clint's voice had been enough to unleash a torrent of gunfire.

Clint let go of the big man and slipped away before he could be caught. That left the big man to his own devices, but he was also under a whole lot of fire. Rather than try to chase Clint or signal his partners, the big man dropped down and covered his head with both hands. Considering the lead flying all around him, it was the smartest move he could have made.

The gunfire tapered off quickly enough. A few seconds later, George hollered, "I get you, Adams? What about your darkie friend?"

"It's just me, you stupid son of a bitch!" the big man cried. "Adams ran off already."

A man stood up and George started walking toward him. The moment George opened the cylinder of his pistol to reload, the man who'd just gotten to his feet aimed his own gun at him.

"You really are stupid," Clint said.

Just then, the big fellow started to get up from where he'd been crouching. Seeing that George had walked toward Clint by mistake, the big fellow stayed down.

"Call your other friend back here," Clint said.

"Why the hell would I do that? Your nigger friend owes me."

"He's got a name," Clint told him as he sighted along the top of his modified Colt. "And I suggest you start using it."

"My other friend's got a name too," George said. "But you don't got to worry about that. He'll introduce himself to that sweet piece of dark meat any time now."

Clint looked toward the cabin and judged the front door was no more than thirty or forty yards away. The third intruder of the night was approaching the door and reaching out for the handle.

"Go on and head inside," George shouted. "I'll be along directly."

Clint watched the third man for a few more seconds, which was just long enough to spot the gun in the intruder's hand. The man tried to open the door, but found it to be locked. He then lifted a foot and opened the door with one vicious kick. Before his foot came down again, Clint's pistol spat one round that hissed through the air to drill a hole clean through that shin. The would-be intruder's leg snapped to the side as if it had been tied to a runaway bronco, spinning the man ninety degrees and sending him to the ground.

Carl stepped into the doorway holding a rifle and a shocked expression that Clint could see even from where he was standing.

"Anyone else want to try and force their way into that man's home?" Clint asked.

The big fellow remained on his knees and raised both hands up over his head.

George was chomping at the bit to take Clint up on his offer, but didn't quite have the sand to see it through. Instead, he fell back to the one thing he knew he could do well enough. "You're all dead!" he blustered. "That n—"

Clint cut that short by thumbing back the hammer of his Colt. The modified pistol didn't require the movement, but the metallic click was loud enough to get the job done.

When he spoke again, George acted as if he was forcing each word out through his teeth. "Carl, his sister, and you, Mister Adams. You are all dead. Ain't nobody gonna stand for their kind treatin' hardworkin' men like this."

"They didn't do a thing," Clint said. "It was all me, and I'll be glad to explain myself to anyone you'd like. I'm pretty certain there are plenty of folks around here who'll believe you and your friends are a bunch of back-shooting idiots."

George may have been too frightened to say anything else, or he may have simply been unable to dispute Clint's words. Whichever it was, he started walking toward the house without another threat or complaint.

"Leave him," Clint said. "Just go and we'll bring your friend back to Pace's."

George showed his true colors that night. Not only did he turn and run, but he left his partner without a second thought.

SEVENTEEN

Just to be on the safe side, Clint slept at Carl's house that night. He actually didn't get much sleep at all, since the only place for him to stretch out was in an old rocking chair in the sitting room. He had blankets to keep him warm, and even a pillow, but none of that was enough to make the wooden slats more bearable upon his back and shoulders. After it was too late to even try to sleep any longer, Clint realized he would have had better luck lying on the ground.

"You're up bright and early," Sadie said as she shuffled from her room and into the kitchen.

Rather than air out a few truthful complaints, Clint nodded and rubbed his neck. "The sun's up, so I am too."

"Will you be staying on then, kind of like our own personal scarecrow?" When she saw the expression on Clint's face, Sadie laughed and shook her head. "Never mind me. After hearing all the fire and brimstone my brother was saying last night, it's a wonder the world hasn't ended by now."

Clint watched her move about to prop open some windows and collect a few cups to go along with the kettle in her hand. She still wore her sleeping gown, but wasn't as careful to wrap it around her. She must have been comfortable around Clint, because she went about her business without making certain every lace was cinched up or checking that her collar was properly situated. She wasn't exactly putting on a show, but Clint did get a few glimpses of her smooth, dark skin.

Sadie's generous breasts swayed beneath the single layer of cotton and the cool morning air made her nipples stand erect against the material. The bright sunlight even shone through her gown when she stood in just the right spot, allowing Clint to see a hint of her full, rounded hips.

"You don't seem too concerned with what happened," Clint said.

She set down the cups and kettle to pick up a dented pail. "If they come back, we'll figure out a way to deal with them. If someone different comes around, we'll deal with them too. Whether all of that happens or none of it, no good will come from us carrying on about it."

"I suppose that's true enough."

"You want some coffee?"

"That'd be—"

"Then go get some water from the pump," Sadie cut in. Before Clint could get a word in, she was pushing the pail into his hands. "No free meals around here, mister. Go on."

The tone in Sadie's voice left no room for discussion, so Clint hurried outside with the pail in his hand. Not only did he spot the pump, but he also found Carl out there with an old Army model pistol in his hand. "What've you got there, Carl?" he asked as he approached the pump and hung the pail off the spout.

Carl rolled the cylinder against his palm and studied the pistol carefully. "Just seeing if I can still remember the old lessons."

"Someone taught you to shoot?"

"Yes, but it was a long time ago."

Working the pump, Clint asked, "Was it your father? Maybe your uncle?"

Carl had a faraway look in his eyes as he slowly shook his head. Finally, he straightened his arm and fired off a shot. "He was a soldier by the name of Abrey. Fell along with plenty of other good men at Ream's Station."

Allowing the pail to fill, Clint squinted and chewed on what he'd just heard. "Ream's Station. Isn't that in Virginia?"

"Yes, sir," Carl replied as he fired off another shot.

The pistol sounded like it was fairly well cared for, but more as a keepsake than an effective weapon. Clint's ear picked up little creaks in the mechanism and subtle crackles and such within the shot that would have slipped past anyone who wasn't proficient with repairing guns of all makes and models. The pistol was old and had seen plenty of use. Scorching along the barrel and the general wear along the trigger guard and hammer told Clint that it had been put through its paces and may have even seen some serious action.

"Wait a minute," Clint said as he leaned forward to get a better look at the gun in Carl's hand. "Ream's Station. Wasn't there a battle there during the war?"

"Yes, sir. Brigadier General August Kautz and his men were cut off and forced to retreat into Petersburg by the damn Confederates." Pausing to sight along the top of the barrel, Carl glared at the tin can he'd set up as if he were looking into the eyes of the devil himself. He fired a shot that clipped the can just well enough to send it spinning off the post.

"That was back in sixty-three?" Clint asked.

"Sixty-four. June twenty-ninth."

Now Clint looked at Carl with even more scrutiny than he'd used to study the gun. "But you don't even look as old as me. How would you know about a battle like that?"

" 'Cause I was there."

"I don't think so."

Carl turned toward Clint, and, for a moment, it seemed

he might take a swing at him. "I was there, Mister Adams. Don't try to tell me any different."

"So . . . that'd make you . . . thirty-five? Forty years old? Either you've got one hell of a baby face or General Kautz mustered up some awfully young soldiers."

Slowly, Carl's stern expression shifted to one of tired resignation. "Mind that pail."

Clint spun around to see water flowing over the side of the pail and spilling onto the ground. As he stopped pumping to place the pail onto the ground, Clint heard another shot crack through the air.

"I wasn't a soldier," Carl explained. "I was a stupid kid who wanted to do anything he could to help the soldiers that got me, my aunt, and my uncle out of Georgia and into Virginia. My uncle said we had to lay low, but I saw a group of General Kautz's men march by one day and I tagged along.

"I don't know how I managed it," he said with a shake of his head, "but I talked fast enough to convince them to keep me on as a drummer. Some of the officers must have thought I was with one of the cooks and some of the other men must have thought I was an orphan with nowhere else to go. However I managed to stay on, I did, and I was so proud. Had something of a uniform and everything."

"So you marched with the men into battle?" Clint asked.

"Not on the front lines, of course. I stayed with the bugler and watched the flags wave as the regiment moved along. I used to think I was making all those feet stomp on account of my drum. Seems foolish now, but I was doing my part the best I could."

Clint had plenty more he wanted to ask, but couldn't help noticing the haunted look in the other man's eyes. He may have only been a boy at the time, but Carl had still seen the war firsthand. The subject wasn't something to be discussed in the same way someone might reminisce about a hard summer.

Those thoughts were in Clint's mind as he brought himself back to the present. Knowing that little bit of history made him even angrier that a loudmouthed idiot like George would try to put Carl through even more hell just because he thought he could get away with it.

"So your soldier friend taught you how to use that pistol?" Clint asked.

"He taught me how to use it without shooting my own toe off," Carl replied. "I'm no gunfighter, but I suppose I should be ready to stand up for myself and Sadie if those men come back after the tournament and all."

"You've got two more shots left," Clint said. "See if you can pop that tin can into the air."

"How'd you know how many shots I have?"

"Whenever you use a gun, you always need to know how many shots you have. Always. If other men are firing, you should count their shots as well. It steadies your nerves by giving you something simple to do and gives you an idea of where you stand during a fight. Even if someone like George is shooting off something other than his mouth, you need to know what you're up against. Odds are, when the shooting starts, most anyone will be too flustered to keep track of something as simple as that. If you do, you'll be one up on them."

"Why are you telling me all of this now?" Carl asked.

"Because you're a good man and you shouldn't have to flinch whenever an asshole like George and his bootlickers look in your direction. I won't teach you to be a killer, but I'll tell you a few things that should make George think twice before giving you so much grief."

Carl smiled and nodded. "All right then. Let's get to work."

EIGHTEEN

The next round of the tournament wasn't set to start until that evening, which gave Clint some time to put Carl through his paces. It wasn't nearly enough time to pass on a lifetime of experience in living by the gun, but it allowed Clint to try and set Carl on the right path. They fired off several rounds and Clint even used some tools from the shed to make some adjustments to the old Army model pistol. The single-action sidearm was a relic compared to Clint's modified Colt, but it held up well over the past twenty years or so.

After having some coffee and oatmeal, Clint and Carl went straight back outside to set up a row of bottles and cans in a makeshift shooting gallery. Not long after that, the calm morning air was shattered by the sounds of gunshots and shattering glass.

Carl had a good eye and listened to everything Clint told him. After a few hours, he was able to pick out targets and hit them well enough to make his mark. But there were things he needed to know that were much more important than why he should squeeze a trigger rather than pull.

"I hope George does come around here again," Carl said anxiously. "I bet I could send him running away like a scalded dog."

"Probably, but you might not have to let things get that far."

Carl shook his head and fired another shot. "You've seen him, Clint. He's not the type to lose interest once he sinks his teeth in."

"He's a coward and a blowhard. I may not live around here, but I've never seen him make a move when he wasn't surrounded by other people to back his play."

"What about that first night you were here?" Carl asked. "He came at me on his own then."

"And he backed off real quick. I'd wager he either thought one of his friends was nearby or that someone else in Pace's would come to his aid. Either way, I know why he keeps coming after you."

"Yeah," Carl growled. "He knows any black man will be strung up before a white man will be scolded for beating him down."

"That may be the case, but it's simpler than that," Clint said. "George is like any other dumb animal. He comes after anyone he thinks is weak, and you might as well carry a sign around your neck that tells the entire world that's what you are."

Carl turned with a fire in his eyes that Clint had only seen there once before. He gripped the old pistol in his hand and looked damn close to using it. "What did you just call me?"

"I didn't call you weak. I said that's what you're showing to everyone else." Although there was a slight change in Carl's eyes, Clint knew the spark was still there.

As if sensing the anger in her brother, Sadie stepped outside to check on them. Almost immediately, she asked, "Are you all right, Carl?"

"See how you're looking at me now?" Clint asked. "The way you're standing. The way you've got your shoulders thrown back. All of it's a hell of a lot different than the way you skulk about town. I can tell the difference right away, and so can your sister."

"I sure can," Sadie replied. "Maybe you should hand that gun over."

"No," Carl snapped. Collecting himself right away, he spoke to his sister in a gentler tone when he added, "Mister Adams is just proving a point. Go back inside."

Clint waited until Sadie was headed for the cabin, then said, "You don't have to strut like the cock of the walk. I understand if you'd rather not draw so much attention to yourself, but you can't scurry with your head down and your shoulders hunched as if you're expecting to be kicked. When men like George see that, they'll just want to kick you."

"A man that looks like I do can't afford to challenge anyone."

"I'm not talking about challenging anyone," Clint told him. "I'm talking about holding your head up and meeting people's eyes. You don't have to stare anyone down, but you don't have to look away from the slightest glance. You can be quiet without muzzling yourself."

"I guess I never thought of it like that," Carl admitted. "I just wanted to keep to myself and go about my own business. I've never been one to give a damn as to what folks think of me."

"And you don't have to give a damn about it. I'm talking about what you think of yourself. If you think you're weak and defenseless, that'll show. No man can afford to let something like that show. This country doesn't tolerate a man that doesn't have the spine to stand up straight."

Carl nodded and stood up straight. Unlike the other times when he'd pulled himself up that way, it seemed he wouldn't go back to slouching anytime soon.

NINETEEN

Once again, Pace's Emporium was filling up. This time, the players were in their seats well ahead of time and none were playing their own side games. They sat around, buying each other drinks and talking about the highs and lows of the night before. At least, that's what they were doing on the surface. The real story was in the way their hands never drifted from their chips and their eyes never stopped sizing up the other men at their table. Each one of them waited for a reason to lunge at the man across from them.

Under any other circumstances, it would have seemed wise to disarm so many gamblers. Then again, the fact that every last one of them had their weapons at their side kept everyone in check. If one of them got too anxious or tried to make the wrong move, all hell would break loose.

It was the most sociable standoff Clint had ever been a part of.

Carl sat at his station next to Delilah, but even she could tell there was a difference in him. Every so often, she would look over and ask him something. Carl responded with a few words and a comforting smile, which only served to confuse her even more. Sitting behind his chips, Clint merely shrugged when he got the questioning look from her.

So far, George was nowhere to be found.

Mister Pace announced the start of the next round with all the usual fanfare. He then stepped back and let the cards be dealt. Even though almost half the gamblers had been eliminated, all of them remained to watch the tournament. In fact, Pace's was even more crowded since the theater had shut down for the night to let its audience watch the winner rake in the final pot. The tournament may not have been the biggest Clint had seen, but it was the only show in Trickle Creek.

"I'll knock you out of this thing, Adams," Mack said from across the table. "Sooner rather than later."

Clint chuckled and gathered up the cards he'd been dealt. "The only way you could knock me out is with a shovel. Even then, I wouldn't recommend you try it."

The whole table laughed at that as the betting commenced. Mack was taking no prisoners this time around, and quickly caught Bull in a clumsy bluff. The big fellow was eliminated and Wendell was next to go. Play was halted for a few minutes so the tables could be rearranged so there were no more empty seats. Amid all that shuffling, Clint almost didn't hear the front door slam open.

"I want that nigger arrested!" George shouted as he and one of his friends stomped inside.

Clint stood up just as George pointed a finger in his direction.

"Him too!" George said. "Arrest 'em both!"

Mr. Pace walked forward and was immediately flanked by a barkeep and Les. The hulking guard placed his hands upon the guns holstered at his side, but looked at George as if he was about to forsake the firearms and just bite his head off.

"Who the hell are you trying to order around?" Mr. Pace asked. "Sheriff DeFalco is still in Dodge City."

"Then get a deputy," George replied. "Hell, we don't need any deputies. Somebody help me chain this . . ." He stopped on his own as if he could feel the angry stares being leveled at him. Forcing himself to speak in a somewhat quieter tone, he said, "Someone help me take Carl out of here so he can be locked up where he belongs."

"And why would anyone do that?" Pace asked.

"Because that's what we do to murderers."

"Who was killed?" Clint asked.

George gnawed on the inside of his cheek and fumed for a few seconds before admitting, "No one as such, but a friend of mine was shot. You should know, since you was there!"

"That's right," Clint said. "I shot him."

Whoever wasn't paying attention to the argument before, surely was now. Even the men at the tables near the back of the room turned in their chairs to get a look.

"A group of men came in the middle of the night," Clint explained, "and tried to attack a defenseless woman in her own home."

One of the girls who served drinks almost dropped her tray. "Someone attacked Sadie? Is she all right?"

"She's just fine," Carl said. "Thanks to Mister Adams."

George stormed toward Delilah's faro table, but Carl surprised him by stepping forward to meet him halfway. Stopping short, George studied Carl as if meeting him for the first time. "My friends were shot and I'm lucky to be in one piece," George said. "Someone should toss both the men that did it into a damn cage."

"Did anyone see what happened last night?" Clint asked. "Right outside this establishment, you and your friends jumped Carl while he was walking away."

Mack was quick to speak up. "I saw it. Some big fella tried to stab Carl in the back."

"I saw that too," another gambler said.

"Where's your wounded friend now?" Clint asked.

George looked around, but could only find the one follower he'd brought with him. "He's lying down. He's hurt."

"Not dead," Clint pointed out. "Hurt. Considering how bad you boys are at staging an ambush, you wouldn't believe how hard I had to work to keep from killing all three of you!"

That sent a ripple of laughter through the gambling hall.

George stabbed a finger at Carl. "The fact remains that that one cheated me."

"Prove it," Mr. Pace snarled.

"I don't got to prove a damn thing. Just look at him."

"I beg to differ, sir," Pace said as he sidled up to stand between George and Carl. "If you're leveling that sort of accusation at someone under my employ, you'll damn well need to prove it."

Like any animal, George knew when he was backing himself into a corner. "I ain't insulting you, Mister Pace. I was cheated, that's all."

"Cheated in my place? I won't tolerate that kind of talk, no matter who's saying it. Prove your claim or take it back."

"I . . . I didn't . . . I can't . . ."

"Can't prove your claim?" Pace said. "Then get out."

"But I'm still in the tournament," George whined.

Pace snapped his fingers to the hulking guard beside him. "Refund his entry fee and see him out."

Les only had to reach into one of his pockets to pull out a wad of cash. He peeled off seventy-five dollars and handed it to George.

"But how can this be?" George asked. "That man is a cheat and I'll see him arrested for it."

Mister Pace looked over to Carl as if he was studying a horse he was considering buying. Clasping his hands behind him, he said, "That man's hardly said more than a dozen words since I hired him and he's never been accused of a thing. As for being a cheat, I would have discovered that by now on my own. From what I hear, you know all too well that Carl has my trust where money is concerned.

He knows better than to steal from me or any other man in here. If you can't prove your claims, I suggest you get your ass out of my establishment."

Holding his entry fee in one hand while still pointing the other at Carl, George looked too flustered to move. "I . . . but my friends . . . I insist that . . ."

Turning on his heels while waving dismissively, Mr. Pace said, "Les, show this man outside."

When the massive gunman took hold of George, it was unclear whether or not he intended to toss George through the door or the nearest window.

TWENTY

George left Pace's Emporium, but he didn't do it quietly. Every step of the way, he cussed and shouted about being treated unfairly and how Carl had cheated him out of what was rightfully his. Clint and Carl followed along behind Les, but none of them was too concerned with what was being said. They were more interested in what George and his friend would do once they were outside.

"This is bullshit!" George snarled as he wheeled around to face his escort. His friend stood next to him, keeping his hand within a few inches of his holstered pistol. "The sheriff is gonna hear about this!"

"I'm sure he will," Mr. Pace said from the doorway.

Squaring his shoulders to all three men, George smirked and said, "You got five seconds to make this right. Toss that cheat out, and Adams along with him, and all is forgiven."

Clint didn't like the way George said that. More importantly, he didn't like the confident glint in George's eye once he'd picked his spot in the street.

"One," George announced.

Looking up and down the street, Clint could only find a few locals gawking at the display. Other than that, George and his friend seemed to be alone.

"Two."

Clint looked back at Carl to see if he knew anything more than what was right in front of them. Carl's eyes were fixed upon George and his hand wavered over a spot close to his belly. Apparently, he'd smuggled in the old pistol under his jacket.

"Three."

George's friend was obviously armed, but they were outnumbered. The last time they'd been in a fight, they cracked like dry twigs. Unless they'd grown an extra set of balls, those two must have some sort of advantage that Clint didn't know about. He only had two more seconds to figure it out.

"Four . . ."

Make that one more second.

Just as George was pulling in a breath to shout out the number five, Clint spotted the reason why those two blow-hards were so confident. "Across the street," Clint announced. "Second window, top floor!"

When Carl and Les spotted the figure in that window, everything went to hell. The next few seconds seemed to tick by a little more slowly as they all went for their guns. The man in the window already had a rifle to his shoulder and was looking down at Pace's Emporium. Clint didn't need to see much to figure the rifleman was the friend of George's who'd been wounded the night before.

Clint lifted the modified Colt from its holster so quickly that he had enough time to pick his target. The man in the window was his first choice, but George and the man beside him were also skinning their weapons. Those two weren't fast enough to be the biggest concern, so Clint went along with his gut instinct.

The modified Colt bucked against Clint's palm, sending two quick shots up to the window across the street. He wasn't sure who else was in that second-floor room, so he did his best to be as accurate as possible. Both bullets found their mark without shattering any glass or even nicking a window frame.

The rifleman jerked up and back as hot lead ripped through him. His finger clenched around the trigger to send a wild shot into the large wood sign directly over Pace's main entrance.

George cleared leather and pulled his trigger, but was in too much of a rush. His round punched a hole into the muddy ditch that ran along the side of the street.

The man standing at George's side drew his pistol in a smooth, fluid motion. Les was just a bit faster, however, and he unleashed a torrent of lead from both of his guns. The massive guard stood his ground and kept his arms so steady that they barely seemed to register the kick from his twin pistols. For any other man, it would have been a waste of ammunition. For Les, however, it made for one hell of a sight. It was also the last sight George's friend ever saw.

Carl's hand got snagged on his jacket when he attempted to take out the gun he'd tucked under his belt. He was fresh from a day of lessons from Clint, which meant he kept his eye on his target and his head clear. Even after George took his shot, Carl fired back with one of his own that dropped his target onto the street.

"Son of a bitch!" George grunted as he hit the dirt on his back. His weapon was forgotten as soon as it slipped from his hand. He winced when he grabbed his hip and found the messy wound there. "He shot me! I told you that bastard was no good!"

"You shot at him first," Les said calmly. "We all saw it." Turning toward Clint, he asked, "Did you take care of the one across the street?"

Now that the two in front of him were down, Clint ran to the building that the third man had used as a lookout point. "One way to find out," he replied. "Keep an eye out for any more."

"Probably won't be necessary," Les said while holstering the gun in his left hand. "George don't have any more friends."

The building across the street was a boardinghouse. Clint pushed open the door and nearly stampeded over a slender old woman wrapped in a heavy shawl.

"Upstairs!" the woman said. "I heard the shot come from upstairs. I swear I didn't know he was going to shoot anyone."

Clint bolted up the staircase with his gun held at hip level. Once he reached the second floor, he turned toward the side of the house facing Pace's and found two doors. One was open to show an empty room and the other was closed. After taking one lunging step, Clint lifted his boot and slammed it against the closed door to knock it open.

The door swung inward a foot or two before it was blocked by something heavy. Clint shouldered it open a little more to get a good look inside. Sure enough, George's other friend was lying on the floor, curled into a ball. Clint might have thought the man was dead if he hadn't grunted in pain as the door knocked against the side of his head.

"Looks like you're gonna need some more bandages," Clint said.

TWENTY-ONE

George was still cussing as the town doctor patched him up. Of course, being shackled to a ring set into the wall of the sheriff's office didn't help his mood any.

"I'm chained up and that black asshole goes free?" George snarled.

"You'll wait there for the sheriff," a young deputy said.

Clint, Carl, and Les stood outside. From there, they could look down the street to watch the wagon roll by carrying the fresh corpse to be planted in the side of a hill just outside of town.

"I suppose I'll be locked up soon enough," Carl said.

Les chuckled and shook his head. "Not by that deputy. He was knocked out of the poker tournament and seeking comfort in the arms of one of our working girls when the commotion started. Mister Pace agreed to keep that bit of information from Sheriff DeFalco in return for a little leniency where you're concerned."

"I won't stand trial for all of this?" Carl asked hopefully.

"No reason for any trial," Les replied. "George saw to that himself. There're plenty of witnesses to see what happened. You'll probably sit in front of the judge, say your piece, and let a few witnesses say theirs. After that, George and his pal will get what's coming to them."

Clint looked at the saloon guard and said, "You sure know a lot about this."

Les shrugged and shifted his hat toward the back of his head. "I've handled plenty of shootings and such for Mister Pace. They all end pretty much the same way."

"Will it be over by the end of the tournament?"

"Should be."

"Fine. That's as long as I'm staying."

"Any time you want to go, just tell Mister Pace," Les said. "I'd wager he'll owe you for pulling this particular set of thorns from his side."

Clapping Carl on the shoulder, Clint said, "Then he should extend that same courtesy to his employee. He did a hell of a job."

Les stared at Carl for a second or two and then slowly nodded. After that, he walked over to George and began roughly going through the man's pockets.

Squirming, but unable to stop Les from searching him, George yapped, "What the hell are you doing?"

When he pulled his hand from George's pocket, Les was holding the entry fee he'd refunded earlier. "Taking this back. One of your shots damaged Mister Pace's property."

"I didn't shoot anything but the ditch!"

"And Mister Pace owns everything from his half of the street, all the way past the lot out back of the Emporium. This," Les said while tucking the money into his shirt pocket, "should cover the damage just fine."

Clint led Carl down the street and back toward Pace's. "You going to be all right?" he asked.

Carl thought that over for a second and seemed mildly surprised by what he came up with. "Yeah. I believe I will."

"How does it feel to stand up for yourself?"

"Good. Real frightening, but real good."

"I'm glad," Clint told him. "Just don't make a habit out

of it. If George has any more friends or decides to take another run at you when this blows over, just meet him head-
on and he'll back down."

"You think I may have to kill him?" Carl asked.

"I doubt it'll come to that. He's hurt and has his back
against a wall. All he's got left is a bunch of tough talk and
hot air."

"So . . . what now?"

Clint nodded toward the Emporium, which was nearly
filled up as if it was just another night of drinking and gambling. "Now I go in and finish playing while you go back to
work."

About twenty paces away from the Emporium's front
door, Carl stopped. He looked at the wide entrance, up at
the weathered sign, and then up a bit farther to the sky
overhead. He sighed and almost looked ready to drop back
into his familiar slouch. "There's gonna be hell to pay."

"What?" Clint asked.

"For all of this. There's gonna be hell to pay and I'll be
the one who'll have to pay it."

As much as Clint wanted to get back inside, he wasn't
about to leave Carl behind in such a state. "Everyone
knows George brought this on. He's even pissed off Mister
Pace, and I don't think that's a man anyone should cross.
George has dug a deep enough hole for himself that he
shouldn't waste more time bothering you."

"I'm not exactly thinking about him," Carl explained.
"I'm talking about the folks who don't like the notion of
someone like me taking a stand against anyone."

"It wasn't just you," Clint told him. "Both Les and I
stood with you. It's over. Unless you start anything else,
it'll stay over. You're not about to go around shooting this
town full of holes, are you?"

Carl smirked at that. "No."

"Then sit back and let George dig himself into a deeper
hole. The more he talks, the worse he'll make it for himself.

An idiot like that doesn't need any help where that sort of thing is concerned."

"I suppose you're right."

When they got back inside Pace's, Clint and Carl were already old news. The tournament was rolling again and gamblers were in the heat of their own private battles. Clint sat back down at his table and Carl sat down at his.

The tournament lasted until a little past one that morning and ended with a hand between Clint and a local man who'd proven to be one of the luckiest men in town. His luck ran out when Clint called a bluff and took every last chip he had.

"We're rich," Delilah said as she rushed up behind Clint's chair to wrap her arms around him. "Time for you to get your prize."

"I think Mister Pace needs to collect the money before handing it—"

Pulling Clint from his chair, she dragged him toward a back room and said, "I've got my own prize in mind."

"Hey!" Mack shouted.

It took every bit of strength Clint had to plant his feet and break Delilah's momentum. "What is it, Mack? Aren't you happy with third place?"

"To hell with third place. I want another crack at you, and I don't mean in one of these penny ante tournaments. I hold a real game, and the next one's to be held in a month or so. Come back if you want to play for some real stakes."

Delilah tugged impatiently at Clint's arm and even let out a few anxious groans while attempting to drag him toward the back room. He wouldn't be able to hold his ground much longer. Considering how excited Delilah was, Clint didn't want to put her off for long.

"What kind of stakes are we talking about?" Clint asked.

"Let's just say your winning here wouldn't even be enough to buy you a seat."

"A lot of gamblers know about your game?"

"Enough to make a few players damn rich," Mack said.

Clint nodded and allowed himself to be pulled away. "Count me in," he shouted over his shoulder.

The Emporium was alive with music, loud complaints from tournament losers, and boisterous stories from the men who'd come close to winning. The winner of the big game remained out of sight for a while, listening to some throaty groans that weren't very loud but were spoken directly into his ear. When Clint and Delilah finally emerged from the back room, she was tousled and he looked as if he'd gotten his prize several times over.

TWENTY-TWO

FIVE WEEKS LATER

When Clint had left Trickle Creek, it was the afternoon following the tournament and the whole town was still buzzing about all that had gone on during the game. The streets were crowded and spirits were high. Clint's pockets were padded with a few extra dollars and Eclipse was trotting upon a new set of shoes.

When he returned, things couldn't have looked more different.

Not only were the streets empty, but the air was stagnant and thick. Some of that could have been explained by the time of day or heat of the season. But those things couldn't explain the discomfort Clint felt as he rode down the street. A few faces looked out through some nearby windows, but seemed more like shadows passing over solid rock.

The town was more than just quiet.

It felt dead.

There were no banners or stagecoaches lining the streets, but that wasn't a surprise since there wasn't a poker tournament going on. The game that had brought Clint back to Trickle Creek was a private affair. Still, he thought he might see more folks out and about doing their normal business.

When he did spot a local who met his eyes, Clint tipped his hat.

That local promptly averted her gaze and turned away.

He couldn't see any lawmen around, which wasn't much different than the last time. He'd heard the sheriff's name mentioned once or twice, but never did lay eyes on the man.

Just a little over a month had passed, but Clint couldn't help feeling like it had been longer. Every inch of Trickle Creek felt dried up and barren. By the time he got to Pace's Emporium, Clint would have welcomed the sound of George's whining voice if only to break up the monotony.

Inside, Pace's was a bit on the empty side, but otherwise fairly close to how he'd left it. Mr. Pace was seated at a small table in the corner farthest from the door, and Les stood directly beside him. Only a few card tables were in use and one of them was for a game of solitaire. One faro game was being run, but not by Delilah. Since she wasn't at her table, neither was Carl.

"Well, look who's back," the bartender said. "Spend your winnings so soon?"

"No. I thought I'd come back to build them up a bit more, though. Where's Mack holding his game?"

"Hell if I know. Ask him yourself when he stops by. That's been closer to eight or nine o'clock. Care for a drink in the meantime?"

"Not yet. When's Delilah coming in?"

The bartender looked at Clint blankly.

"Delilah," Clint repeated. "You know. The tall beauty who runs the faro game?"

"Yeah. I know who you're talking about."

"Well, where is she?"

After steeling himself a bit, the bartender told him, "She's gone. We buried her not long after you left."

TWENTY-THREE

Clint was lunging across the bar to grab hold of the tender's shirt before he knew what he was doing. "What did you say about Delilah?" he snarled.

"You mean you haven't heard?"

"No," Clint replied. "Why don't you tell me."

Judging by the look on his face, the bartender was reluctant to deliver that bad news again after the way Clint had reacted to it the first time. Unable or unwilling to form the words, the barkeep merely opened and shut his mouth like a trout that had accidentally flopped into a boat.

Just as he was coming to his senses, Clint felt a heavy hand settle onto the back of his neck. The thick, meaty fingers didn't cut off his air, but they flexed as if to let Clint know they could do so without any trouble whatsoever.

"What's the matter, Clint?" Les asked as he tightened his grip just a bit. "Did you just hear some bad news?"

While Les might not have threatened him directly, Clint got the other man's intent well enough. If he didn't quiet down quickly, Les would be forced to quiet Clint down himself. Letting go of the barkeep, Clint retreated to his own side of the bar. Pulling out of Les's grasp, he turned to the guard and said, "I think you know damn well what I just heard. Is it true?"

"A lot's been going on since you left. You'll have to be more specific."

"Delilah." Just saying her name brought Clint's eyes to the faro table where she'd dealt her game. At that moment, the table looked twice as empty as the other ones that weren't in use. Now that the wind was out of his sails, Clint asked, "Is it true that she's gone?"

Les nodded solemnly. "She was killed a little while after you left."

"Who did it?"

"Perhaps we should do this somewhere a bit more private."

"What do you know about this?" Clint asked. "What aren't you telling me? Just spill it."

"I'm not gonna hide anything from you. I just said we should talk somewhere else. You want to come along? Fine. If you want to tear things up in Delilah's name, you'll have to do it somewhere else."

Clint let out a breath. "Last time I was in town, I barely heard you string three words together."

"That was back when you were another gambler I had to watch. You were also just another man locking horns with George and his asshole partners. Things change once you stand side by side with someone while there's lead flying around you. Besides, if you were anyone else who'd grabbed hold of Jerry like that, you'd be eating the bar instead of leaning against it right about now."

Clint glanced at the barkeep and saw the man nod. "It's true," Jerry said. "I seen it, and it ain't pretty."

"Come on," Les said as he draped a muscular arm across Clint's shoulders and steered him toward the back of the place. "Mister Pace would like to have a word with you."

TWENTY-FOUR

Mr. Pace's office was small, but lavishly decorated. The little patch of floor space was covered by a fancy rug and every wall was hung with paintings and even a few photographs documenting the Emporium's rise from little saloon to its current state. In a room that could very well have been the size of two large closets combined, the desk situated in the middle of it seemed big enough to push three grown men straight outside. Seeing Les fill up a corner like a giant's coat rack was damn near comic.

Mr. Pace sat behind the desk, rolling a cigar between his thumb and forefinger. "Care for one?" he asked.

Clint shook his head.

Deciding not to fill the cramped room with smoke, Pace motioned to one of the two chairs in front of his desk. "Why don't you take a load off?"

"I don't want a cigar and I don't want to sit," Clint said. "I want to know what happened to Delilah."

Pace put the cigar in his mouth and reached for a match from one of the many shiny little boxes on top of his desk. He grabbed a stick, tapped it against the desk, and seemed to consider striking it despite what he'd decided a few moments ago. Clenching his teeth to the point that he looked ready to bite clean through the cigar, he said, "George shot her."

Clint barely had time to tense his muscles before he felt Les's hand on his shoulder again. Shaking loose once more, he snarled, "What the hell kind of law do you have in this town? George was supposed to be in jail!"

"He was in jail. He was about to get carted away to a bigger jail a few towns south of here when he got loose and decided to get himself some payback."

"Got loose, huh?" Clint scoffed.

"Well, some folks raised a stink on account of George being locked up on the word of a colored man." Before Clint could jump in again, Pace held up a hand and added, "There were other people speaking up on Carl's behalf. Plenty of others around here had a problem with George. I'm one of them. That's how we got George taken care of without a trial. Sheriff DeFalco came back to town, heard from all concerned parties, and decided to ship George off to rot in a cage built to hold him for a good, long time."

"Then he escaped?" Clint asked.

"From what I hear, he was given a day to get his affairs in order before being ridden out of town. One of the deputies was along with him when he was allowed to say goodbye to his ma. Sometime that day, George got away from the deputy."

Clint furrowed his brow and scowled as if choking on the smoke that would have been spewing from the thick cigar between Pace's teeth. "Do all your prisoners get such good treatment?"

"I own a saloon, Adams. I'm not the law around here. If you want to know why the sheriff or his deputies did what they did, I suggest you ask them."

"I might just do that." Clint turned and found himself facing a solid wall of muscle. Looking up into Les's eyes, he asked, "You mind getting out of my way?"

Les didn't budge and he didn't respond to Clint's question. He simply shifted his head a little to look at the other man in the office.

"Delilah was here when she was shot," Pace said.

Clint turned around to face the desk.

Now that he saw he had Clint's attention, Pace went on. "She was at her table, doing her job, when the bastard came barging in here waving a gun around. He screamed about how he was railroaded and cheated and all that other bullshit he normally spouts."

"Don't you hire men to take care of situations like that?" Clint asked as he shot a glance over his shoulder.

"I was about to tear the son of a bitch in half when he threatened to start shooting," Les said. "About a second after that, he pulled his trigger anyway."

"It happened just like that, Adams," Pace verified. "And just as quick. I don't have to tell you what a slippery, fucking little coward George was. You shouldn't have any trouble believing he'd take a shot at a woman to save his own skin."

"Was?" Clint asked. "So he's gone?"

"Gone as in not around here anymore," Pace replied. "Any more than that . . . who's to say?"

"So when was Delilah shot?"

"George said he wanted to kill Carl and anyone else who meant to put him behind bars," Pace explained. "Carl stepped up to speak for himself and Delilah stepped up to stand with him. I don't let Carl carry a gun while he's working, but Delilah usually had one handy. I don't know if she got to it or not before George shot her."

"She didn't," Les said. "George got spooked the longer he was here and then he fired at Carl. Either he's a piss-poor shot or he meant to kill Delilah, because he put a bullet right into her heart."

Hearing those words hit Clint like a punch to his chest. Even though he'd been told the basics, having it laid out so plainly for him like that was tough to swallow.

Les may have felt the same thing, because his voice wavered slightly when he continued speaking. "George was gone before Delilah hit the floor. I took off after him, but he could've gone anywhere."

"What about the law? Aren't they looking for him?" Clint asked.

"Like Mister Pace said, you'll have to ask them for yourself."

"And like I said, I'll do that very thing unless you intend on keeping me locked up in this room."

Pace tapped his cigar against his desk. "I have a lot invested in this place, Mister Adams. I can't afford to have folks driven away. George has done enough damage, but he hasn't been heard from since. For all we know, Carl got to him."

"Did Carl go after George?"

"Could be. We haven't seen him, either. My point is that I don't want to have you kicking up any more dust in my place. You're welcome to stop by. After what you did the last time you were here, you can sleep, eat, and drink here without spending a cent. I know Mack wants to hold his game and I'll even offer a private table for it without taking my usual percentage."

"How generous of you," Clint grumbled.

"It is generous, Mister Adams. You're upset right now, so you may not be able to see that so clearly. Just don't spit in the face of my generosity by conducting any more rough business in my Emporium. I know you and Delilah had a . . . shall we say . . . especially friendly relationship. If you intend on paying anyone back for what happened to her, you have my blessing. She was a good woman and a wonderful dealer. I've never had a game where so many men were so willing to buck such shitty odds on such a consistent basis."

Pace stood up and pointed his cigar at Clint. "If you want to gun somebody down, do it outside. If you want to beat to a pulp someone who had anything to do with what happened or has any connection to George, do it some-where else. You understand me?"

Despite the fact that Pace had raised his voice to a threatening snarl, Clint found it easier to deal with him. It did him some good just to see someone else get riled up while talking about George. "I understand. When you say I have your blessing, does that mean you'll back me up if I need it?"

"As long as you don't cross the line," Pace replied as he extended his hand across the top of the desk, "most defi-nitely."

Clint shook Pace's hand. Only after that did Les step aside to let him walk through the door.

TWENTY-FIVE

The first time Clint had been in town, he'd thought the sheriff's office had been an abandoned building. The windows had always been dark and the structure sat without a sign of life within its quiet walls. Now it was one of the few parts of Trickle Creek that actually looked to be thriving. The windows were no longer covered. A light shone from inside. A few shadows even moved around in there. It seemed the town's justice wasn't completely dead after all.

When Clint opened the office's front door, he was greeted by a lanky kid in his late teens who wore a deputy's badge on his vest. The kid might have wanted to say something, but he didn't get the words out before Clint walked right past him and toward a balding man securing a wanted notice to the wall.

"Sheriff DeFalco?" Clint asked.

Just as he'd suspected, the balding man turned around to answer.

"That'd be me."

"I'm Clint Adams."

The sheriff thought about that for a second and then grinned. "The fella who won the tournament? Congratulations. I trust Pace handed over your prize money."

"Yes, he did. I came to talk about one of his faro dealers."

"Please don't tell me you were cheated."

Resisting the urge to kick over the sheriff's desk, Clint said, "No. I mean Delilah. You know . . . the one that was shot in front of half the town."

"I wouldn't say half the town, but it was quite a spectacle."

"And what are you doing about it?"

Sheriff DeFalco turned around to make sure the notice he'd just put up was straight. Then, he settled into his chair and hooked a thumb toward the newest addition to his wall. "See for yourself."

The notice he'd hung advertised a five-hundred-dollar reward for the capture of George Willem. Other than a sparse description of George's crimes, the only thing on the notice was a hastily drawn sketch of the fugitive. Even after all the times Clint had seen the man, he barely recognized the picture as George.

"That's it?" Clint asked. "Do you at least have a posse going after him?"

"All right, then. Say I round up a posse. That should only take a week or so to find enough men willing to sign on for a long ride away from home and hearth. Once I get my men, I do what?"

"Look for George," Clint snarled.

"Do you happen to know where we should start?" DeFalco asked. "Do you know where he went? Do you even know in which direction he might have gone? There's a lot of open country out there, Mister Adams."

Clint pulled in a breath to steady himself. He'd ridden on enough posses to know how much work it took to form one. He'd also hunted down plenty of wanted men, so he knew that was no easy task. He'd also dealt with his share of lazy lawmen, enough to know when one was dragging his heels on purpose.

"Just about everyone who knows George hates the bastard," Clint said. "Rounding up a few to hunt him down shouldn't be too hard."

"And after that?"

"Don't you know how to track someone? For Christ's sake, you've got to at least know a tracker. Is this all you do when someone escapes from you? Kick your feet up and hope they cross your path on their own?"

The sheriff cocked his head as if he was about to tell a slow child why they should wipe their nose. "Don't tell me how to do my job."

"Maybe someone should start by telling you to *do* your job!" Clint roared. "After you get off your ass, we'll worry about how."

DeFalco was on his feet quicker than Clint thought he was capable of moving. "You want to see me do my job? Why don't I knock you on the skull and toss your sorry hide into my jail for disrespecting a keeper of the peace?" After a few seconds passed without either man making a move, the sheriff said, "George is a pathetic piece of shit, but I won't waste my time chasing after him while he runs and hides in a cave somewhere. As long as he stays out of my town, it's just as good as if he was in my jail."

"This is because his problem was with Carl?" Clint asked.

"Most folks around here would demand I run that darkie out of here just for taking a white man's money at that faro table."

"And what about Delilah?"

"Her death is a shame, but I've heard enough to convince me it was an accident. You may not like to hear this, Mister Adams, but she was also a whore who spread her legs any chance she could get." Grinning ever so slightly, DeFalco added, "I hear you know plenty about that."

Clint didn't approve of hurting a lawman, but he wanted to knock this one out so badly, he could taste it.

"Did you know Delilah was brought in more than once

for cheating?" the sheriff asked. "Do you happen to know how she got the charges dropped and went back to work without so much as a blemish to her name? Want to guess how many dicks she sucked to earn enough money to buy all those fancy dresses when other dealers can barely feed themselves?"

"That's enough, Sheriff," Clint said. "I've found out all I needed to know."

"Good. Don't come back around here expecting me to waste my time and money on a posse when this town is better without that whore and her shifty bean counter. George is gone and he won't come back. That's the end of it, and I don't want to see you in my office anymore."

"Don't worry," Clint said. "I sure as hell don't want to see your face again, either."

TWENTY-SIX

From what he'd seen of the job Sheriff DeFalco did when he was on his game, Clint knew he was better off without having to worry about the lawman getting in his way. If DeFalco wanted to sit in his office and do nothing, that just cleared the way for Clint to do his own work unimpeded.

Somehow, no matter how many times Clint told himself things like this, they didn't make him feel any better. More than anything, he'd wanted to bury his fist into that pompous lawman's face. It wasn't as if the greasy bastard could have stopped him. Even his deputies weren't any kind of threat. The only thing that stopped Clint was his own common sense.

Knocking a lawman on his ass was just too much trouble. No matter how much it would be worth some time in jail, Clint wasn't about to give DeFalco the pleasure of locking him up. Unlike the town's law, Clint had a job to do.

He didn't bother going back to Pace's Emporium, or anywhere else in town, for that matter. Instead, Clint rode out to the one spot where he thought he might get some honest answers. Sure, the people doing the talking may not be completely impartial, but he doubted they would leave such a bad taste in his mouth.

Eclipse took him to the cabin on the outskirts of town in no time at all. By the time Clint was swinging down from the saddle, he was getting the first glimpse of his welcoming party.

"You get right back on that horse and keep riding!" Sadie demanded as she stormed out of the cabin with a shotgun in her hands.

Clint raised his hands, but didn't make a move to climb back onto Eclipse's back. "I'm not here to bother you two. Just give me a chance to prove it."

Slowly, she lowered the shotgun from her shoulder. "Clint Adams? Is that really you?"

"It sure is."

"You don't have to prove anything to me. Come on inside."

Eyeing the shotgun, Clint asked, "You sure it's safe?"

Sadie shook her head as if she'd just realized the shotgun was still in her possession. Taking hold of it by the barrel, she walked into the cabin and propped the shotgun against the wall right next to the door. Now that her hands were both empty, she rushed to Clint and gave him a strong, almost desperate hug.

"I'm so glad to see you!" she said. "Of all the folks I thought would come here, I wasn't expecting one of them to be you. I can't tell you how happy I am!"

After catching his breath from being squashed like a grape, Clint rubbed Sadie's back and told her, "I was hoping to find you, but after talking to some people in town, I don't know if you should be here."

Sadie was a full head shorter than Clint, but was very strong for her size. When she let go of him, she straightened his shirt as if to make up for nearly cracking his ribs. "Where else would I be? This is my home."

"Yes, but . . ." Rather than frighten her with the things he'd heard, Clint bit his tongue. "Where's Carl?"

"Lord knows."

"You don't know where he is?"

"Nobody does," she said. "And I hope it stays that way."

TWENTY-SEVEN

During his previous visit, Clint hadn't spent a lot of time with Sadie. For the most part, she'd been checking in on them while he and Carl practiced with the old Army model pistol outside. She'd stayed out of their way and tended to her own affairs. Now, she paced the kitchen area as if she didn't know quite why she was there. Her simple brown skirts swirled around her as she kept scrambling from one spot to another.

"Will you sit down?" Clint asked. "You're making me nervous."

"Nervous? You can't be half as nervous as I am."

"Then sit down and tell me about it."

She stayed still for a moment before she looked ready to jump out of her skin. "Do you want some water? I want some water."

"Sure. Let's both have some water."

Now that she had something to keep her hands busy, she calmed down a bit. Once he saw her hands had stopped trembling, Clint asked, "What do you know about Carl?"

"Just that he's off trying to hunt down that murdering bastard that shot poor Delilah."

"He's going after George?"

She nodded and brought two cups of water to the table where Clint was sitting. Setting both cups down, she lowered herself onto a chair and let out a slow breath. "He went to the sheriff, but that lazy pig isn't good for anything but taking up space. He even went to Mister Pace, since he's known Delilah ever since she came to town. But do you know what that rich man said to Carl?"

"That hunting down a killer wasn't good for his business?"

"More or less. He said it was the law's concern and that getting involved in something like that would reflect badly on the Emporium. Carl did all of this the day after George came up missing. He even tried to see about hiring bounty hunters to go after that man so he could get the justice he deserves."

"So Carl headed out on his own?"

Sadie averted her eyes and bit her lip. She took a sip of water, but that didn't seem to help loosen her tongue.

"You can tell me," Clint said. "I can help."

"Sure, that's what I thought about the others that were supposed to help. I even went to have a word with the sheriff myself. You want to know what he said to me?"

Clint took a sip of water, if only to try and douse the fire that was building inside of him. "No need to tell me. I was just there myself and heard more than enough."

The intensity in Sadie's eyes told Clint that she was dying to tell her story anyway. She'd already gotten mad enough as it was, so she might as well burn as hot as she could get. After taking a sip of water for herself, she thought better of it. "Nobody here gives a damn about poor Delilah. At least, nobody that's in a spot to do anything about it. That's why Carl went off to do what he can. After what you told him," she added with a glare, "he wanted to charge straight out and drag that killer back by the scruff of his neck."

"After what I told him?"

"You know what I'm talking about. All of that fooling about with that dusty gun, shooting those cans, like that would make him into a soldier."

"I wasn't trying to make him into anything," Clint protested.

"Is that a fact?"

"Yes."

"Then what were you trying to do?" she demanded.

"All I told him was to hold his head up and stop walking around with his tail between his legs. Folks may look at you differently around here, but that doesn't mean he has to think any less of himself."

"You don't know what the hell you're talking about! You can walk into any town you want and be the mayor if you set your mind to it. Or you can just go about your business without anyone giving you any grief. That's not so for us, Mister Adams."

Clint pulled in a deep breath and then took a drink. When he was sure Sadie had finished talking, he told her, "One man's circumstances may be different than another man's. They may be drastically different. But every man needs to stand up straight and hold his head up. Do you honestly think I was telling him to pick up that gun of his and risk his life trying to fight a killer?"

Though she was trying to hang on to her anger, Sadie quickly had to let it go. Actually, she simply lost the steam she needed to keep charging ahead the way she'd been doing. Finally, she closed her eyes and sighed. "You shouldn't be the one hearing all of this, Clint. I'm sorry. It's just that . . ."

Since Sadie didn't have enough wind in her sails to complete her sentence, Clint did it for her. "It's just that there's nobody else around here to holler at."

She snapped her eyes open and let out a tired laugh. "More or less. You must think I'm—"

"I think you're frustrated and angry with what's happened. Talking to Sheriff DeFalco is enough to do that to just about anyone."

"I still shouldn't have said those things to you. Whatever you said to Carl made him a changed man. Everyone thought so. On one walk to the store, I must've had a dozen people come up to me and ask what had gotten into him. They said he looked like he was the one who'd won that tournament."

"And you don't have any idea where he is?"

She shook her head. "I sure don't."

"When was the last time you saw him?"

"It's been a day."

Clint thought he must have misunderstood what she'd just told him. After thinking it over for a second, he couldn't figure out what else she could have said. "What was that?" he asked. "Did you say it's only been a day?"

"Right around there."

"I thought all of this happened weeks ago. Everything I've heard led me to believe that Carl's been missing for just about that long."

"As far as anyone in town knows, that's right," Sadie replied. "But Carl comes back to check in on me every now and then. He's worried someone will come after me when they think I'll be here all by myself. Maybe one of George's friends or kin will come to try and . . . well . . . I'm sure you can imagine."

"If you're worried about that, why stay here?" Clint asked.

"Carl told me to leave as well, so I'll tell you the same thing I told him. This is my home and I won't be chased away from it." Softening a bit, she added, "Also, Carl comes back to check on me. I wasn't lying before. I don't know where he is right now, or even if he's alive. But if he didn't have me to worry about, he'd be out there without any reason to come back."

"When's he due to pay another visit?"

"Sometime tomorrow, I hope," Sadie replied.

"Would you mind if I stayed here to wait with you?"

Suddenly, Sadie looked as if she was ready to cry. "I'd like that."

TWENTY-EIGHT

It wasn't long before Clint needed to try and find something to do to make himself feel useful. Since he'd decided to stay with Sadie, she'd been a constant blur of motion. If she wasn't fixing a meal, she was straightening a room of the cabin. If she wasn't doing any of that, she was carrying things back and forth from one of the sheds outside. Even when she sat, she was either knitting or mending some piece of clothing that belonged to her or her brother.

Every time Clint offered to help with something, she refused. He didn't insist too strongly, because she was obviously happy to have someone to talk to while she kept her hands busy. Finally, Clint found the one chore that she wasn't so keen to do on her own.

"Why don't I chop some firewood?" he asked.

She started to reach for the axe leaning against the wall, but nodded and said, "If you don't mind."

"Watching you bustle around here is making me feel like a bump on a log."

"You've been tending to your horse and—"

"Just let me get to work," he interrupted. "Otherwise, you'll just talk yourself into doing it."

She followed Clint outside and stood a few paces away

as he rolled up his sleeves and set the first chunk of wood onto an old stump. "Didn't you have some other business to take care of?"

Clint dropped the axe well off of center, which resulted in a thin sliver separating from the wood. "What do you mean?"

"Did you know about this whole mess before you got here?"

"No."

"Then why'd you come back to Trickle Creek?"

Clint hefted the axe over his head and dropped it down on target, so two pieces of kindling flew onto the ground. "One of the men from the tournament is holding a game and I meant to play in it."

"When will you be going?"

He halved another piece of wood and picked up yet another piece in a rhythm that became more solid with every movement. "I won't."

"Carl won't be here until tomorrow. He may not be on a strict schedule, but he sure won't be early. Every time he comes back, it takes him longer to arrive, so I can guarantee he won't be here tonight. You should go to your game."

"And leave you here alone? I don't know about that."

She waved that off easily enough. "If nobody's come for me yet, than nobody's likely to. Besides, I don't think anyone in town will want to help George do anything."

Clint chopped another piece of wood in half before asking, "What about those two that were with George the last time I was here? Do they have friends around town?"

"I don't even know who those two were."

"What about their names?" Clint asked, thinking he might be able to do some asking around to see if there might be anyone else in town who could be on George's side.

Sadie scratched her chin and then said, "I can't even think of their names. You know, I don't think I ever heard mention of who those two were."

"So much for that idea," Clint grumbled.

Walking up beside him, she asked, "What was that?"

"Nothing," Clint replied before dropping the axe through another hunk of wood. "I'd rather not leave you alone. Not until I find out more about what's going on around here."

"I've got a shotgun in the house, Clint. I can handle myself." Reaching out to pat his shoulder, she added, "Carl and I fended for ourselves this long. We can do it for a bit longer."

Clint propped the axe upon the edge of the stump and worked a kink from his shoulder. "I've had my fill of that town. Besides, it's not like Mack will miss me at that game. I never even sent word ahead of when I'd arrive."

"Fine, then. We can stay here." So far, Sadie's hand had yet to leave Clint's shoulder. She rubbed his muscles through his shirt and let her eyes drift along the spots where sweat had soaked through to cause the material to stick to his skin.

As Clint looked over at her, he found his own eyes wandering down along the smoothly curving lines of her body.

Suddenly, both of them forced themselves to look in another direction. Clint couldn't help thinking about what Carl would say if he knew a man was looking at his sister that way. Judging by the flustered look on her face, Sadie was thinking along those same lines.

"Then again, maybe getting away from here would be a good idea," Clint said. "Care to join me at that game?"

"That sounds like a good idea."

TWENTY-NINE

"We really don't have to do this," Clint said as he escorted Sadie down the street. After spending a good portion of the day trying not to watch her, getting away from that cabin seemed like the most proper thing to do. Normally, propriety wasn't too high on Clint's list, but he didn't want to take advantage of a woman in her situation.

Of course, it was clear that she was watching him just as much. At times, she seemed to be watching him even harder.

"You can't promise a lady a night on the town and then back out as soon as we get here," she scolded.

"Well, this town has become pretty dangerous."

"And it'd be that way whether you were here or not. Since I never intended on hiding in that cabin, I would have been walking down these streets sooner or later. Having you with me makes me feel safe," she said as she tightened her grip around Clint's arm.

They were halfway down the street when Clint stopped. "Aw, hell."

"What is it?"

"I just remembered that Mack's game is being held in Pace's Emporium."

"That's where all the big games are held," Sadie replied. "At least, that's what Carl always used to say."

"I'm sorry. You must not want to go anywhere near that place."

Although Sadie maintained a brave front, she wasn't able to keep it up all the time. When she looked at the front of Pace's Emporium, the easy smile that she'd been wearing became frayed around the edges. The vibrant glow that always came from her eyes dimmed for a second, and it looked as if she was having trouble pulling in her next breath.

Suddenly, all of that passed.

Sadie straightened up and said, "You told my brother to walk proud and hold his head high. You were right about that, Clint. He always walked as if he was expecting a beating. Sometimes it broke my heart to see someone so strong act so weak. I've got to do the same."

"This is different," Clint said. "This isn't about being weak. It's about you not wanting to go in there so soon after—"

"No," she snapped. "It's not about being weak. It's about me walking straight into that gambling hall when everyone in this town, Mister Pace included, expects me to run away or hide up in that cabin." She cinched her arm around Clint's and showed him a genuine smile. "I want to see the look on all those faces when they see me walking in there with you."

After hearing the things Sheriff DeFalco said about Carl and Delilah, Clint could only imagine what was said to Sadie's face when she'd gone around asking all those same questions. Besides that, if anyone was out to attack Sadie for any reason, they'd probably look for her at her cabin. Clint knew the layout of Pace's pretty well and could watch her just as well there as anywhere else.

"All right, then," Clint said. "Promise to stay close to me."

"There isn't anywhere else I'd rather be."

Her answer had come so quickly that it seemed to surprise her. Sadie flashed a broad smile and fell into step beside Clint, as if to say it was a pleasant surprise indeed.

They walked into Pace's together, arm in arm. Among the people there to watch their entrance was Sheriff DeFalco. The moment he got a look at the pair, he shook his head and walked for the door. Once he was gone, the place took on a much more welcoming feel.

"Good to see you, Clint," Mack said as he approached them. "I was starting to think you weren't going to show."

"You should be so lucky," Clint said.

"Who's your friend?"

"Sadie Malloy," she said before Clint could introduce her.

Mack nodded appreciatively and took in the sight of her. She'd dolled up for the evening in a dress that was one of the better ones she owned, but not nearly as silky as the ones worn by most other ladies in the room. "Will you be joining us this evening? I know Clint will need all the good luck he can get."

"Is that the table where we'll be playing?" she asked as she pointed to a large table that was sectioned off from the room by a partition that had been set up to keep bystanders to a minimum.

"It certainly is."

"Then I'll most definitely be joining you," she said.

As he followed Mack toward the back of the room, Clint figured Sadie was talking so much to put on a good appearance. He didn't think much of it until she began dragging her feet and slowing him down like an anchor that had been hooked to his elbow. When he was practically brought to a stop, Clint asked, "What is it? Do you want to leave?"

"You see that man back there?" she whispered. "The one getting up from the table?"

Clint looked at the table where Mack's game was being held and couldn't miss the portly gentleman wearing an expensive suit struggling to wriggle out from between his chair, the table, and the wall. "Yeah. What about him?"

"I think he knows something about what happened when Delilah was shot."

Clint could tell the man wanted to get away from the table, but he could very well have needed to visit an outhouse. "What makes you think that?" he asked.

"His name's Tom Naderman, and usually he's always got a kind word for me. Carl told me he'd been getting friendly with George while building up a whole lot of debt at the tables. Since he's running like a rabbit instead of looking at me, I'd say he's got something to hide."

Now, Clint looked over to Sadie. "Is there anything else you want to tell me?"

She shrugged and said, "I've lived here for years. You want me to tell you everything I know about everyone?"

"Well, come on. Let's see if ol' Tom's got anything to say."

THIRTY

Mack protested the moment he saw Clint steer away from the table, but wasn't about to follow him and Sadie to the door. Fortunately, Tom Naderman wasn't a small man and probably couldn't have gotten away at a dead run with a ten-second head start. Even with Sadie in tow, Clint got to him before Tom made it to the door.

"Evening, Tom," Sadie said cheerfully.

Tom whipped around and sucked in a breath. "Oh, uh, evening Sadie. Who . . . ahhh . . . who's this with you?"

"You know Clint. He won the last tournament."

"Oh, yeah. I think I recall that."

"You were in it," Clint said. "I just remembered, you were sitting at one of the front tables and were knocked out early."

Tom nodded and backed toward the door. "That's right. What can I do for you?"

While Clint may have had his doubts about Sadie's hasty assessment of why Tom was squirming away from the poker game, he didn't have any now. Everything from the shifting of Tom's eyes to the fresh streams of sweat trickling from his forehead advertised the fact that he was hiding something and was nervous as hell about it.

"Where are you going?" Sadie asked. "Weren't you gonna say hello?"

"Sure I was," Tom said with a shaky laugh. "Just . . . uh . . . needed to step outside to answer the call of nature."

"Outhouse is on the other side of the building," Clint pointed out.

"Oh. So it is. Guess I'm a little nervous."

"Still in your slump?" Sadie asked. "Carl told me you were into Delilah for a whole lot of money. He mentioned you and she had some unfriendly words after the tournament."

"I don't know what you're talking about."

Clint could tell Sadie was bristling. Rather than let her sink her teeth into the portly man, he eased her back a few steps and said, "Why don't you buy us some beer? After all, we'll be doing our best to win some money at Mack's game and could use all the liquid courage we can get."

Once she saw the intent glare Clint was giving her, Sadie nodded and headed toward the bar. She was still in his line of sight, but far enough away for Clint to speak without being heard. Once he stood toe-to-toe with the other man, they might as well have been in their own locked room. Within seconds, Tom was squirming to get away from him a whole lot more than he'd wriggled to get away from Mack's card table.

"Something tells me you're the sort of man who would rather not look at a woman than admit you took part in getting her brother killed," Clint snarled.

"What?"

"You know she went to the sheriff, right? DeFalco must spout off a lot about something like that. I bet he didn't have many good things to say about Sadie, her brother, or Delilah, for that matter."

"That was him talking," Tom replied.

"But if she went to the sheriff, that means she's trying to drag the law into this mess even more than it already is."

"The law isn't in it. Not anymore."

That told Clint plenty. Since Tom wasn't so nervous anymore, it meant he wasn't trying to lie. It also made it a safe bet that he figured he wasn't in any danger at the moment. Clint didn't have to do much to change Tom's mind about that.

"You know why I sent her away?" Clint asked. When Tom glanced toward the bar, Clint said, "She's the sort of woman who attracts a lot of attention. She's also the sister of a man who's become quite the topic of conversation around here. That means everyone's watching her a whole lot closer than they're watching us. And that means I can do a whole lot to ruin your evening if you don't start talking straight to me, real quick."

"I was just trying to take a piss," Tom whined.

"You were trying to get the hell out of here the moment you laid eyes on me and Sadie. Now that I've heard about you owing money and being on friendly terms with George, that puts all kinds of questions into my head."

"George who?"

Clint's hand snapped out to push Tom's back against the wall. It didn't take a lot of force to shove the man back an inch or two, but Tom nearly jumped out of his skin.

"George doesn't have a lot of friends," Clint said. "The two I saw with him aren't in very good shape. From what I can tell, folks around here don't even know the names of those two. Maybe that's why you bolted for the door when you saw us."

"No, that's not it."

"Then why?" Clint snapped.

While Tom fumbled for his words, he glimpsed toward the empty table where Delilah and Carl used to work. "If you've got something to say about Carl, then say it," Clint demanded.

Tom shook his head and stammered some more.

When Tom shook his head this time, he did it as if his life depended on it. Clint was definitely on the right track.

"I knew Delilah," Clint said. "But only for a few days. You can say whatever you need to about her."

Glancing about nervously, Tom saw that nobody was paying them any attention. Sadie was in the middle of a heated conversation with the bartender, which drew even more attention to her. Les was nearby, watching the argument the way he watched everything else in Pace's. Since the only one watching him seemed to be Clint, Tom let out the breath he'd been holding and started talking.

THIRTY-ONE

"I didn't do anything, I swear," Tom said.

"Then why were you running?"

"Because you and Delilah were close."

"She was a faro dealer," Clint said. "Winners will love her and losers will want to kill her. You strike me as a loser."

Like any man who'd come to Pace's to sit in on a game held by a professional like Mack, Tom took offense to that last statement more than anything else that had been said so far. His nostrils flared and his eyes narrowed as though he might stand up to Clint right there. He didn't quite have the backbone to follow up on that, however.

"I lost my share," Tom said. "I lost plenty, but I was winning again. I was winning big."

"So why would you have anything against Delilah that you wouldn't want me to hear?"

"You don't know?" Tom snarled.

Clint was about to demand that the other man stop trying to steer the conversation in the wrong direction, when he realized he was the one who wasn't keeping up.

"That . . . woman put a wager on you during the tournament," Tom said impatiently. "She bet with money that wasn't even hers that if you won, her debts would be cleaned out."

"So you won enough to pull yourself out of a hole . . ." Clint said.

"Out of a hole and back into a profit," Tom cut in. Just thinking about that was enough to give him the strength to fight for a bit of distance between himself and Clint. He shoved Clint back a step, but then immediately regretted it.

Since they still looked like they were just having a normal talk, Clint nodded and didn't make Tom pay for stepping out of line.

"That bitch owed me a healthy chunk of cash," Tom said. "No offense if you were sweet on her."

"Go on," Clint told him.

"It took a whole lot of work to get out of debt, especially with how easily she pulls a man into playing one hand after another."

Faro was a dollop of skill wrapped in a whole lot of luck. On top of that, a talented dealer could make any player seem as if he was on the verge of striking it rich. Delilah was talented at a lot of things, and dealing faro was most definitely one of them.

"I was on a streak," Tom mused. "First I got flush, then I got ahead. Then I got ahead even more until that damn dealer started trying to push me off onto one of the other tables. I think that black fella was a good luck charm for me. Too bad he's as good as dead."

"Watch your mouth," Clint warned.

As soon as Tom saw the angry fire in Clint's eyes, he went back to the petrified state he was in a little while ago. "She made the offer to me and a few others that were ahead of her game at the start of the tournament. She watched you play that first game with George and got real confident you could win. She even pulled a few strings to try and get you to sit in that same chair so she could watch you play."

Clint smirked at that. From the first instant, when Delilah had gotten a good angle to peek at George's cards, she'd been scheming to use it to the best possible advantage. Perhaps she'd been trying to steer him one way or the other for some reason, but Clint didn't care. No matter what angles she'd been working, she didn't deserve to be shot dead in her own saloon.

"She seemed distracted and desperate to find any way to get her bet going on the tournament," Tom explained. "When Mister Pace heard what she had to say, he wasn't too happy about it. Then, she proposed a deal to me and some of the others who'd been wringing her dry. If her pick to win the tournament actually won, she wouldn't owe us anything. If you didn't win the tournament, she'd owe us double."

The more Tom talked about the bet, the less nervous he became. It was the difference between a man dreading going into a battle and a man remembering how he'd lost that battle. The latter was a much more tired and resigned affair.

"I thought about turning down the whole bet," Tom continued. "I may have been one of the last holdouts. Then she got even more confident and offered to pay out triple what she owed if you lost. If you won, we'd have to pay her half of what she owed us."

"Triple, huh? Those are pretty good odds."

Brightening up at the first sign of a sympathetic ear, Tom nodded. "Yeah, they were. With so many others in that tournament, and with all the things that could go wrong in any game, we figured she was just trying anything she could to get out of her debt. Me and one of the other fellas in on the wager thought she'd be desperate enough to fuck us to get out of paying up."

Speaking from personal experience, Clint said, "That must have been tempting."

"She was a pretty lady," Tom sighed. "But you won and I was put right back where I started. In debt to Delilah. I had plans for that money she owed me. Even if she paid me in pieces here and there, it would have gone a long way toward settling my debts in other spots around town."

"All of that goes down the river when I win the tournament, so you decide to get some payback on Delilah," Clint said.

Tom shook his head. "I didn't know what was gonna happen to her. Honest, I didn't. George asked if I wanted a chance to earn some money to make up what I lost, and if that came with a chance to make her look bad, then so be it. She wasn't supposed to get shot. That was never part of the deal."

"Wasn't George in jail?"

"He was let out to tend to his affairs every so often," Tom explained. "Most of the times he drank himself stupid or bedded down with some whore, but he spent a lot of time here."

Clint felt anger flush through his skin to make his face hot and his fists clench. It seemed Sheriff DeFalco was either one of George's best friends or he was simply one of the laziest lawmen in the country. Either way, Clint wanted to have another word with him. Taking out those frustrations on Tom, however, wouldn't do anyone any good.

Sadie was through arguing at the bar and was waiting patiently for her drinks, so Clint hurried up and asked Tom, "What was the deal you had with George?"

"I was supposed to figure out when that table was stocked with the most cash," Tom said. "I play there so much that I'm damn near rooted to one of those chairs. George told me what to look for and how Delilah or that dark-skinned fella would act when they were sitting on a lot of money."

"How would George know those things?" Clint asked.

"I don't know, but he did. He said to watch for the big wins or the big losses. Then he told me how to spot when Carl was getting ready to take a bunch of money to the safe in back. I passed on what I saw and a day later, George comes in with guns blazing."

Clint narrowed his eyes as if he was staring through to Tom's soul. "Was she really shot by accident?"

"Yes," Tom said instantly. "She was trying to grab Carl and pull him behind her table. It was a mistake."

"All right then." With that, Clint turned and walked away.

"What now?" Tom asked.

"Now we play some poker."

THIRTY-TWO

Since Sadie insisted that her brother wouldn't try going to the cabin until late morning or early afternoon, Clint rented a room across the street and down a ways from Pace's Emporium. That way, they wouldn't be sleeping somewhere that had already been attacked by the same man who was on the loose. Also, Clint could simply look out the window to get a good look at the front of Pace's.

If anyone was coming up the street, he could catch sight of them.

If anyone made it into the small hotel he'd chosen for the night, he could hear the stairs squeak.

If someone got through all of that, they would have to kick down a door and come in awfully quick to avoid catching a bullet from Clint's modified Colt.

"Did you see the look on that old man's face when you asked for a room?" Sadie chuckled as she opened the drawers of the bureau situated against the wall. "I swear he looked like he was about to throw a fit."

"Do you know him?"

"I believe I've seen him once or twice."

"Then he's probably afraid I'll take you up here to steal your virtue," Clint said.

Despite the fact that both of them knew what the old man was shocked about, Sadie said, "That must be it. We probably could have just stayed at that game until it was time to wait for Carl. It didn't show any signs of stopping when we left."

"We've been playing cards for almost eight hours. Any longer and I wouldn't be able to see much of anything other than the inside of my eyelids."

"Are you telling me the great Gunsmith can't play cards all night long?" she chided.

"Not when I'm also watching you as well as all the doors in Pace's and everyone inside. If we stay in one place, it'll just make it easier for someone to come after us."

"You still think someone is after me? Wasn't I right about Tom?"

"Sure," Clint replied. "He knew plenty, but he didn't know everything. George is still out there. He's desperate and dumb as ever, which means we can't predict what the hell he might do. A man like that doesn't even try to make sense. That's about the only thing that makes him dangerous."

"You could kill him on sight." Narrowing her eyes, Sadie added, "I could kill him just as easy."

"I'm sure you could. All the more reason for us to get some rest instead of playing poker all night."

Sadie's mood brightened when she dug her hands into the pockets of her skirts and pulled out a few small bundles of cash. "If I kept winning, they probably would have kicked us out anyway."

"I doubt it," Clint grunted as he sat upon the edge of the bed and pulled off his boots. "I lost more than enough to make up the difference."

"We could always go win it back."

"After all that fighting you did with that barkeep, I thought you'd be more tired than this."

"Oh, that was nothing," she said with an offhanded wave. "He made a remark about never serving liquor to anyone of my color and I chewed him out for it." Seeing the expression on Clint's face, Sadie added, "Those were his words, not mine."

"Well, you gave him plenty of your own words while I was talking to Tom."

"I sure did. What did he say, anyhow?"

"I'm still mulling that over. How about I tell you once I've drawn some more conclusions."

"Is that a friendly way of saying you want me to stop pestering you?"

"More or less," Clint replied.

She stood in front of him as Clint sat on the edge of the bed. When Sadie looked down at him, her hair fell over her shoulder to brush against his face. Reaching out to tug at the buttons of his shirt, she asked, "What about now? You still want me to stop pestering you?"

"Not exactly, but . . ."

"But what? I've been wanting to do this all night long. You might even say I've wanted to do this ever since the last time you were in town."

Clint placed his hands upon her hips to feel the rounded curves of her body. "Then by all means, pester away."

THIRTY-THREE

Even though she was standing and Clint was seated, Sadie wasn't much taller than him. As she worked the buttons on his shirt, Clint moved his hands up and down along Sadie's body. Her round hips flowed down into strong legs, and when Clint reached around, he found a plump, inviting backside.

"There now," she purred. "Isn't that nice?"

"It sure is."

"You've done so much, why don't you just lay back and let me do some work?"

"Work, huh?"

She smirked as she unbuckled his belt and pulled his jeans off. "Well, I suppose that depends on how vigorous you do things."

Looking directly into Clint's eyes, she wrapped her hands around his stiffening cock and stroked him up and down. The harder he got, the wider she smiled. As he grew to his full length, she even looked pleasantly surprised. The surprise became even more pleasant when Clint reached under her skirts to pull down the few garments she wore beneath them.

Her skin was the color of chocolate and was softer than

cream. Every new place he put his hands brought a new
sound from the back of Sadie's throat. Soon, she leaned her
head back and stroked his cock while Clint explored every
inch of warm flesh between her legs. She was damp when
he first touched her down there, but was nearly dripping
wet by the time he rubbed the sensitive nub of her clitoris.

"Oh, Lord," she moaned. Gathering up her skirts, she
kept them up above her waist so Clint's hand could move
freely. Sadie even spread her knees apart and straddled his
legs as though she were riding a horse.

Clint was having a hell of a time watching the expression on her face turn from arousal to something much more
intense. She clenched her eyes shut tightly and reached out
to grip his shoulder with one hand. As her lower body
started to tremble, she pumped against his fingers in short,
quick little motions.

When Clint curled his fingers inside of her, he knew the
exact moment he found her sweet spot. Sadie tried to say
something, but could only get out a few choppy grunts before drawing a deep breath and holding it. Her grip on his
shoulder tightened and she bit down on her lower lip. For a
few seconds, she was completely still. Then, an orgasm
pulsed through her from head to toe and she let out a slow
sigh.

Opening her eyes, Sadie said, "I was supposed to be the
one doing the work."

"Then get started," Clint told her.

She raised her eyebrows at the challenging tone in his
voice and slid her hand all the way down to the base of his
erection. Lifting herself up onto her tip-toes, she positioned
her hips over him and guided his cock between the moist
lips of her pussy. Sadie ground back and forth while slowly
taking him inside. When he was in far enough, she placed
her hand upon his shoulder and eased the rest of the way
down.

Clint grabbed on to her hips and started to pump, but

was stopped when she pressed more of her weight down upon him. Now that he was pinned beneath her, Sadie warned, "I'm the one doing the work, remember? You just sit there and let me do it."

Although Clint wasn't about to let go of her, he loosened his grip so his hands were just resting upon her sides. She wriggled back and forth while pulling her dress up over her head. There was some tugging and squirming involved, but the dress was soon on the floor behind her. Besides that, Clint didn't mind her squirming one bit.

Sadie's body wasn't plump, but she had wide, generous curves. Her breasts swayed with every move she made, and her large, dark nipples soon became hard with anticipation. Clint could feel a tension in her legs which had nothing to do with the way she straddled him. Everything about her, right down to the breaths she took, was excited for what was to come. Fortunately, she didn't make him wait much longer.

Once again resting her hands upon Clint's shoulders, she started rocking back and forth against him. Every now and then, she shifted her weight an inch or two to one side or the other so he moved within her at a slightly different angle. Those subtle motions were more than enough to make Clint become even harder inside of her. Before long, it became difficult for him to rein himself in.

Smiling at the frustration building in him, Sadie mused, "Having a tough time, Clint?"

"On the contrary. Things couldn't be much better from where I sit."

"Well, now." Sadie purred as she slid the palms of her hands from Clint's shoulders down to his chest. "Let's just see what I can do about that."

She rocked a bit more, but also started lifting herself up and down. Using her hands against his chest for support, Sadie built up a powerful head of steam in a short amount of time. It wasn't long before Clint felt like he had to hang on to her just so she wouldn't fall off of him. Of course, she was holding on so tight that it would have taken a hell of a lot for her to lose her grip.

Sadie arched her back and shook her head until her long, dark hair surrounded her face like a mane. Low, rumbling groans came from the back of her throat like growls as she began digging her fingernails into Clint's flesh. That stung for a brief moment, but quickly added spice to what he was already feeling.

Encouraging her with a few little swats to her buttocks, Clint started pumping his hips up into her every time she rocked back. Sadie let out an appreciative moan and leaned back a bit farther. Holding on to her hips, Clint kept her from rocking any more so he could pump between her legs with more force.

Instead of fighting him, Sadie leaned back and supported herself with her hands upon Clint's knees. She spread her legs wide for him and moaned louder as he pounded up into her again and again. Her pussy was slick with moisture now and clenched around his cock as another orgasm started to ripple through her lower body.

Clint didn't say a word as he started to stand up. Following his lead, Sadie climbed off of him and stepped back. Before she could ask what he was doing, Clint wrapped his arms around her and gave her a deep kiss. Sadie was still in the heat of their lovemaking, so she immediately slipped her tongue into Clint's mouth. She even let out a few muffled groans as she felt his rigid penis rub against her.

Holding her in place, Clint walked around behind her. He wrapped his arms around her again, cupping her generous breasts and rubbing against the smooth curves of her backside. Sadie didn't need any more prompting than that to spread her legs again and lean forward to grab on to the chair where he'd previously been sitting. Before she could look back to check on him, Clint was easing into her from behind.

He took the first couple of strokes at a leisurely pace, sliding in and out in a smooth rhythm. Then, Clint gripped her hips a bit tighter and started thrusting in earnest. Sadie bucked against him eagerly. She was so eager, in fact, that she almost tipped the chair over by leaning against it.

"Better move this before we start breaking furniture," she said as she wriggled free of him. She walked across the small room as if she enjoyed every second she was naked in front of him. Then, like a sleek cat, she crawled onto the bed and lowered her upper body so it was resting upon the mattress and her backside was up in the air. "Well, aren't you coming?"

"Just admiring the view," Clint said as he walked over to the bed. He admired her for a few more seconds as she slowly twitched her hips back and forth. He placed a hand upon the small of her back and used his other hand to guide his penis between her thighs. She was wetter than ever, so he slid in without a hitch.

Clint wanted to take it easy, but was unable to hold back for long. Sadie's body fit him like a glove and she knew just when to move or clench her muscles to fit even tighter around him. She moaned in a constant rumble that also got her hands clawing at the blankets. When Clint quickened his pace, Sadie responded by moaning louder and gently rocking back and forth in time to his thrusts.

When he felt his climax approaching, Clint knew better than to hold it back. Everything from the feel of her skin against his hands to the warmth of her body was helping him build into a powerful wave that threatened to explode at any second. He pulled in a few deep breaths and rubbed Sadie's smooth buttocks as he continued to slide in and out of her.

"Just a little more, now," she urged. "Do it harder, Clint. I won't break."

Clint didn't need to be told twice. He grabbed her hips and buried his cock all the way inside her, eliciting a groan of pleasure that seemed to have come all the way from Sadie's toes. He then leaned forward to run his hands along her sides. She rose up and arched her back so she could reach back and slide her fingers through Clint's hair.

For a second, he thought he wouldn't be able to stay inside of her from that angle. But Sadie bent in just the right way to accommodate him. In fact, he felt something completely new as he entered her from that slightly different angle. She liked that angle just as much as he did, because Sadie started breathing heavily and letting out long, throaty moans.

"Good Lord, Clint. That's . . . I never . . . oh, good Lord."

Sadie started to go limp as if her orgasm was leaving her too weak to remain upright. Clint reached around to cup her breasts and keep her in the position that had brought her to such a state. Every time Clint thrust into her, he bumped against her rounded buttocks. When he pushed in a bit more from there, he unleashed something inside of her that sent a powerful quake throughout Sadie's entire body.

Rather than hold her up any longer, Clint eased her down. Sadie laid with her chest flat against the mattress, her head turned to the side and her hips up high to receive him. Her face was twisted in an expression of sheer pleasure, but she didn't have enough strength to make another sound. Clint got a good grip on her and thrust a few more times before he was past the point of no return.

After pounding into her one last time, he unleashed an orgasm that took the breath from his lungs. He climbed off the bed to place his gun belt on the chair within easy reach and when he came back, Sadie was already asleep.

THIRTY-FOUR

Clint slept in the chair that night. He let Sadie have her rest in the bed on her own simply so he wouldn't get too comfortable himself. If he crawled into bed with her, he could very possibly be lulled into too deep of a sleep to catch the telltale signs of someone trying to get into his room. That warm body in between those soft blankets would have been too much of a distraction for a man who needed to keep his ears and one eye open throughout the entire night.

He didn't know if anyone would come after him or Sadie, but then again, he hadn't guessed someone would come after Carl or shoot Delilah. Clint still had a hard time swallowing that cold bit of news. At times when he'd been playing cards at Mack's table, Clint could relax as if Delilah simply wasn't working that night.

Other times, it was difficult for him to stop thinking about how she'd assaulted him with all those nods and shakes of her head that eventually proved to be her way of turning him into a cheat. If anyone else had done something like that, Clint would have never wanted to see his or her face again. More than likely, he would have made them regret even trying a trick along those lines. But Delilah was different. She may have been a cheat, but Clint had the sense that her heart was in the right place.

No matter what, she didn't deserve to die the way she had.

Clint might have been able to accept it a little better if he'd heard that she'd been caught cheating or got into an altercation after stacking the odds a bit more in her favor. That sort of thing happened to crooked faro dealers, and it would have been the sort of thing any dealer in her position would have prepared for. Delilah would have taken a gamble on her own accord and lost.

Unfortunate, but not quite tragic.

But Delilah had died because a loud, crazy idiot had crossed the line. George was too far past that line to be dealt with by the likes of a lawman like DeFalco, and he was too far gone to be left to the mercies of the harsh open country. Someone needed to track George down and teach him why there was a line in the first place.

George must have known that brand of justice was headed his way. Perhaps that's why he'd become so reckless. Clint didn't really care about that bastard's reasons any longer. All he needed to know was that George was nearby and living on borrowed time.

Almost certainly, that's all Carl needed to know as well.

In those hours he sat in his chair, watching the door and listening to every bump in the night, Clint knew that Carl was probably out there somewhere doing that very same thing. If Carl wasn't listening and watching for George to make another foolish move, then there was the distinct possibility that he was making some moves of his own.

George was too desperate to lie low, and he was too stupid to run away.

The more Clint thought about that last part, the more it bothered him. When he put that together with what he'd heard from Tom back at the Emporium, Clint was bothered even more.

The line was going to be crossed again. Clint knew that much for certain. All that remained to be seen was who would stay alive long enough to get back to the proper side.

THIRTY-FIVE

Although they were both anxious to see Carl, Sadie didn't seem to be in much of a hurry to leave the hotel. She took her time getting dressed, possibly as a way to tempt Clint back into bed, which almost worked. If Clint hadn't gotten himself so riled up in his hours of sleeplessly watching the door, he would have had no problem spending a few extra hours there. Once she saw that Clint was too wound up to be tempted, Sadie made herself presentable and followed him to where Eclipse was tied.

"Are you worried about missing your brother?" Clint asked.

"I told you before. Carl shows up later every time. Even if he did get there before us, he'd wait to see me. If he intends on running about trying to get his fool head blown off, then let him cool his heels for a while."

Clint climbed onto the Darley Arabian's back and helped Sadie up into the saddle behind him. "If it's all the same to you, I'd still like to get back there as soon as we can."

"Whatever you like," she said as she wrapped her arms around his midsection.

The ride to the cabin was short, due mostly to the fact that a lot of the town was still sleeping. There was just enough light in the sky to light their way, and the air still had the cool, damp bite left over from the night before. A few locals were setting up shop for the day, but they were too busy to notice a single horse riding past.

As soon as they arrived at the cabin, Clint walked around inside to make sure there were no visitors hidden in the corner of a room and waiting to get the jump on them. Sadie rolled her eyes and crossed her arms as she waited for him to come outside.

"Find any monsters?" she asked.

"No. You can come on in."

"I told you there wouldn't be anyone in there."

"Well, I appreciate you being so understanding," Clint sneered. "With everything that's happened, I would have thought you'd be more cautious."

"A murdering asshole is running about and the sheriff doesn't give a damn," she said as she rummaged in her kitchen to gather what she needed to prepare some breakfast. "An innocent woman is dead. If my brother isn't dead, he's sure as hell trying to get there. Sometimes, the rain comes down so hard that you just can't concern yourself with getting wet anymore."

Clint would have had a hard time arguing with that, so he kept his mouth shut and took a look in Carl's room.

Sadie didn't seem to mind if he snooped around, but he still wasn't about to turn the place upside down. Instead, he opened a few dresser drawers, checked under the bed, and opened the small, narrow closet. Clint wasn't just being nosy. He was looking to see just how long Carl intended on staying away. Since most of the drawers were full of clothes and there was a pair of old boots overturned under the bed, it didn't seem that Carl meant to leave for good. But the overturned boots suggested to Clint that their owner might have left in a rush.

So far, all of that matched what he'd been told.

Clint looked around the cabin's perimeter and searched

the surrounding property, but was unable to come up with any fresh tracks or other signs that would prove someone had been sneaking around there recently.

All of this was helpful, but was mostly to keep him occupied until breakfast was ready. Even after Sadie had put together a simple meal for them consisting of some scrambled eggs and bacon, Clint could barely sit still long enough to eat.

"You're not very good at waiting, are you?" she asked.

"What was your first hint?"

"We could keep busy, you know," Sadie said with a wicked glint in her eye. "My bed's awfully comfortable."

Just as Clint was going to reply to that, he heard the front door creak as if it was being eased open. When he turned to face that direction, Clint's hand reflexively went toward the Colt at his side.

Carl stood in the doorway with a rifle hefted over one shoulder and a holster wrapped around his waist. "What did you just say about your bed?" he asked suspiciously.

THIRTY-SIX

Before Clint could do much of anything, he was cut off by Sadie. She dropped what she was doing, raced across the small cabin, and jumped at her brother to wrap her arms around his neck. Carl hugged her back and even picked her up for a moment to swing her like a little girl.

"It's only been a little while," Carl said. "You're acting like you didn't think you would see me again."

"With you stomping off to wherever you go, I never know if I'll see you again," she scolded. "Please tell me you're going to stay home for a while longer this time."

Carl looked up to meet Clint's gaze. "Can't do that, sis."

Waiting until Sadie had had sufficient time to fuss over her brother, Clint stepped forward. Carl let her go and extended a hand to him. "I hear you've been busy," Clint said as he shook the hand that was offered.

"I didn't even hear you'd be coming back to town. Did my sister find you and drag you back here?"

"Not at all. I came back to play in Mack's poker game."

Carl nodded. "That's right. Mister Pace always gets excited when gamblers with deep pockets decide to use a table in his place. Just another angle he's got worked out.

So," he added as his eyes drifted toward Sadie's bedroom, "it sounds like you've been staying here for a while."

She swatted him on the shoulder and spun around to march back to the kitchen. "Don't be so crude. I was just playing when I said that."

Unconvinced, Carl looked back at Clint with an intensity that could only be summoned by a protective brother.

Clint held up his hands and said, "I swear, I've never seen her bed and didn't plan on seeing it now."

Although that wasn't exactly in the spirit of the truth, it wasn't a lie. Carl must have sensed as much, so he nodded and stopped staring a hole through Clint's skull. "Are you cooking up breakfast?"

"It's a bit late, but yes," Sadie replied.

"I'll have some, if you don't mind."

"Not at all, Carl," Sadie replied as she looked over her shoulder to smile at him. "Welcome home."

"Thanks."

Clint watched the other man carefully. It didn't take much scrutiny to pick out the fact that Carl was tired. He moved as if there were bricks in his boots and breathed as if he was tasting fresh air for the first time. There was plenty Clint wanted to talk about with Carl, but he figured most of it could wait until they'd all gotten some food in their bellies. Some questions, however, Clint couldn't hold back.

"So what happened with Delilah?" he asked.

Carl's head drooped as if he'd been expecting that question all along. "She was shot by an animal that should've been in a cage," he replied.

"I hear she was trying to get to you."

Sadie glanced over at them as she scrambled the eggs. Although she seemed ready to jump in, she kept from doing so.

"I honestly don't know what she was trying to do," Carl said. "One minute George was shouting at me and the next, I was being pulled behind her table."

"What did George want?"

"Same as he always wants. He says he was cheated, even though everyone knows better. He created a commotion and started a ruckus. It was so loud, it just filled my ears and got my head rattling. When it looked like I was on my own, I decided to step in and end it. That's when Delilah must have gotten jumpy, because she was the one to pull me back. There was a shot and she dropped."

"And after that?" Clint asked.

Carl drew a long breath and rubbed his eyes with the back of his hand. "After that, she died. What else is there to say? She was my friend and she was killed for no good reason."

"That's enough, Clint," Sadie said as she began walking to her brother's side.

Without looking at her, Carl waved her off. Sadie got back to her cooking, but looked over her shoulder every couple of seconds.

"What about Les?" Clint asked.

"What about him?"

"Every time I've been in that place, Les is watching over everything like a hawk. Was he there that night?"

After thinking about it for all of two seconds, Carl said, "He's there every night. I think he lives in one of the rooms upstairs right in the Emporium. Come to think of it, I recall him being there that night. There was a rowdy drunk causing trouble at the bar and Mister Pace gave Les hell for not tossing the man out on his ear fast enough."

"That's interesting."

"It is?"

"Most definitely," Clint mused. "I talked to a man named Tom Naderman who said Les wasn't there the night Delilah was shot. Either that, or he wasn't around when it happened."

"Tom Naderman?" Carl grunted.

"You know," Sadie insisted as she brought over some coffee. "*Tom.*"

Carl shrugged and took a sip, which did more to bolster his spirits than anything else so far.

"Even if Les had stepped out for a bit or was upstairs in his room," Clint said, "he should have been able to get downstairs quickly enough to deal with George. How much commotion was there when he arrived?"

"He busted in with his gun drawn," Carl said. "Folks were shouting. People were jumping from their chairs."

"But Les still didn't hear enough to draw him into the main room before things went from bad to worse? That's even more interesting."

"I can beat that, Mister Adams," Carl whispered. Shooting a quick glance at Sadie, he added, "But not right now."

If Carl wanted to wait until after getting something to eat, Clint would oblige him. He'd never wolfed down a hot meal so quickly.

THIRTY-SEVEN

The last time Clint had been standing on the stretch of land just outside of that cabin, he'd been teaching Carl how to stand up for himself. Although shooting lessons had been a part of that, Clint's intention had been to help Carl walk a little straighter. That was it, and that seemed like an awfully long time ago.

Back then, Carl had been quiet and unassuming. Clint supposed he still was those things, but they didn't fit him the same way as they had back then. Now, Carl was still quiet. He just seemed to be seething quietly instead of scurrying like a frightened mouse. That short time ago, Clint certainly wouldn't have guessed to hear the next words to come out of Carl's mouth.

"I nearly killed the men responsible for shooting up Pace's. I had 'em in my sights, but I didn't pull the trigger. Sorry," he added with a deferential look at Clint. "I meant squeeze the trigger."

"What men?" Clint asked.

Carl looked at the cabin and then leaned over a bit so he could see through one of the windows. Once he saw that his sister was still inside, he said, "George, for one. There are some others, but I don't know exactly who they are."

"Friends of George?"

"I don't think so. They were pushing him around pretty good."

"Why don't you want to say any of this in front of Sadie?" Clint asked.

"Because she's a fighter. If someone says so much as a cross word to me or her, she's likely to give them a piece of her mind. She doesn't know what kind of trouble that leads to."

"I think you may be underestimating her."

Carl nodded. "Then she just doesn't care about starting any trouble. I do. I've got to. Women get leeway that men don't."

"That's neither here nor there, Carl. Where the hell have you been?"

"I'm doing what you taught me to do. Standing up for myself and seeing to it that men like George don't just trample all over me. Since nobody gives a damn about Delilah now that she's in the ground, I suppose I'm standing up for her too. Lord knows she deserves it."

"You can't be going too far," Clint pointed out. "Sadie says that you come back here every other day or so."

"Don't need to go far. George and them others are holed up at an old farm a few miles from here. It took some doing, but I followed one of them all the way back to that spot without being seen."

"Are you sure about that?"

"Yes, sir," Carl said with a solid nod. "I'd follow them a ways and back off when they got suspicious. Followed them a bit farther the next time and even farther the next. Once I knew they were going to the old Blair place, I crept in to get a look."

Apparently, Carl's old mouselike habits had their uses after all.

"They're planning something," Carl continued.

"How do you figure that?"

"Because every time I check in on them, they've got a few more horses and a few more guns lying about."

"Could just be that there are more men coming in," Clint said.

"Which doesn't make things any better. They're up at that farm hiding and getting ready for something. Otherwise, they'd be in town where there's hot food and warm beds."

"Do you recognize any of these men?"

Carl slowly shook his head. "Other than George, I've only seen maybe one or two of them in Pace's a time or two. But I can't be certain about that. The more I think about it, the more all those faces tend to blend together. I guess you were right. I should have kept my head up more. Maybe then I'd be of some use."

"I don't know. It sounds like you've been making yourself real useful."

"All I've been doing is following and watching," Carl grumbled. "That doesn't amount to much."

"That depends on if you can get me to that farm without being seen."

"I could do that for certain."

"How good are you with that rifle?" Clint asked, nodding toward the Winchester hanging from the boot on Carl's saddle.

"I'm a pretty good shot up to sixty yards out," he replied. "Any farther than that, I can hold my own."

"Let's get out to that farm and see if we can figure out what George and those others are up to," Clint said. "Here's where all that following and watching will pay off."

THIRTY-EIGHT

Clint might not have considered riding out with Carl if there was any decent law to be found in Trickle Creek. There were a few good lawmen he knew in the neighboring county, but getting to them and bringing them back would take more time than they had. George was an idiot, but even the biggest idiots knew when to run. From what Carl had said, George seemed anxious to do just that. And if the others Carl had spotted really were planning something, there was no way to be certain of how much time was left before that plan was put into motion.

Even with everything working in his favor, Clint knew there wasn't much time before Carl took action on his own. Carl was wound up tighter than a watch spring. The fact that he had a just cause only added more tension. It wasn't long after he and Clint rode away from the cabin that Carl's shoulders began to come down from around his ears.

"You sure Sadie will be all right in that hotel?" Carl asked.

"I spent all night thinking about every spot to watch and every sound to listen for in that room," Clint replied.

"She'll be fine. Also, she's got her shotgun. Anyone walk-ing into that door trying to do her harm won't have much time to regret it."

"I suppose nobody's got a good reason to come after her. All those times I came back to check on her, I didn't find anyone close to that cabin. Whatever it is George and those men are after, it's not Sadie."

"We'll see for ourselves."

They covered a good amount of ground in a short amount of time. Eclipse was well rested and ready to go, but Carl's horse didn't have any problem keeping up. Where Eclipse excelled in pure muscle and stamina, Carl's horse made up in experience. Carl claimed to have blazed the trail from the cabin to the farm himself, and Clint had no reason to disagree.

To the naked eye, the trail looked like any other stretch of flat Kansas grassland. Tall weeds and clumps of trees blanketed an expanse of gentle slopes, rocks, and holes dug by any number of critters. Carl navigated it all with ease. He turned sharply at times, so Clint followed in the same path to narrowly avoid a stump that would have tripped up a less cautious rider. Every so often, Carl would hunker down and tap his heels to his horse's sides to take advantage of a clear shot across half a mile of smooth ground.

Not once in all of this time did Clint see so much as a hint of a real trail. When Carl pulled back on his reins after a few hours of riding, Clint thought it was just to give the horses a rest.

"The Blair Farm is just over there," Carl said as he pointed to the west.

It was the time of day when the sun was on its way down, but not close to the horizon just yet. Clint thought he was looking at more old trees when he was actually seeing the bleached, crooked planks that might have been the skeletal remains of a windmill. If Carl hadn't pointed it out, he might have ridden past without giving it a second glance.

"Doesn't look like there's much of anything there," Clint said.

"Most of it's overgrown, burnt down or just plain rotted away. Most of the town's probably forgotten it's even here."

"Are there any lookouts?"

"Sometimes," Carl replied. "The only ones I've ever seen are posted on top of the old barn. We rode all the way around to this side of the property so we could creep up on the blind side of that barn."

Clint squinted into the distance and shook his head. "I don't see any barn."

When Carl looked over to him, it was one of the few times Clint had seen him smile. "If everything could be spotted from a mile away, why the hell would anyone want to hide there?"

"Good point."

After tethering the horses to a nearby tree, Clint and Carl started walking toward the farm. Carl had a route memorized for that as well. He barely even needed to look down as he dashed through the tall grass and hopped over the various things on the ground that might trip him up. Because he knew exactly where to step, he hardly even made a sound. Clint, on the other hand, wasn't so lucky.

The first time Clint accidentally kicked a rock, Carl shot him a stern backward glance. The second time, Carl let out a hiss that would have put any snake to shame. When Clint stumbled on a tangle of low bushes, he thought the other man was going to tear his head off.

"We're almost there," Carl rasped. "Do you want to have a look or just march in, pretty as you please?"

"We agreed on the first."

"Then hush up!"

Clint wanted to defend himself, but knew it wouldn't do any good. Instead, he lowered his head and scurried after Carl like a dog with its tail between its legs. Carl was too distracted to appreciate the irony.

THIRTY-NINE

After a lot of scrambling through the weeds, Clint and Carl circled around to cross onto the Blair property line, which was marked by a broken-down old fence. The ground beneath Clint's feet took on a smoother feel. Although it hadn't been worked in a long time, the land had obviously been cared for in its day. They didn't have to scurry for much longer before Clint could spot the rest of the structures.

The tallest of those was the old windmill, but that wasn't sturdy enough to stand up to the wind. A man perched upon those splintered beams would have brought it all crashing down. The next tallest structure was an old barn missing most of its roof and loft. The little house was in the same terrible shape. He had heard mention of a fire, but the farm could just as likely have been hit by a twister. Either way, the spread was a large corpse rotting in the prairie sun.

Clint might not have scouted the area as well as Carl had, but he did come prepared. Lifting the spyglass he'd brought from his saddlebag, Clint studied the farm a little more closely. "Looks like there're a few men in that house," he said.

"And don't forget the two in the barn."

Shifting his gaze toward the barn, Clint muttered, "I only see one."

"One in the loft and one inside, watching through the doors."

"I don't see the one on the ground floor."

"He's there," Carl assured him. "Every time I've come here, there've been two in that barn."

"All right. I'll take your word for it." Clint slowly panned the spyglass back and forth. "I count six horses tethered near the house. Could be more tied up somewhere else but I doubt it. Those six are being kept in a spot where they have the best chance of staying out of sight."

"Sometimes they keep their horses in the house," Carl explained. "The whole thing's close to being hollow."

"Is there a second floor or did that collapse?"

"Must've collapsed, because I've seen men leading their horses in and out of there."

"Did you recognize any of those men?" Clint asked.

"I thought I might have seen a few of them at Pace's, but just about anyone who comes to town heads into Pace's sometime or other."

"I recognize one of them."

Carl leaned over as if he meant to look through the same eyepiece as Clint. Even when Clint handed over the spyglass and pointed him in the right direction, Carl still didn't catch on.

"Look through the front window of the house," Clint said. "Big guy wearing the coat. See him?"

"Yeah. He's been there a few times. Always wears that big hat and the bandanna wrapped around his neck. It's tough to see his face."

"Don't need to see his face. Look at the double-rig holster he's wearing. See the way he keeps his hands near those guns at all times? Notice the way he stands like he's filling up as much space as he can?"

"Yeah," Carl said with an inkling of recognition. "I

can't put my finger on it, but I may have seen that man before."

"You don't recognize him because he's mostly covered up in the sorts of clothes he never wears on a daily basis. Those guns are a dead giveaway, though. At least, they are for someone who knows what he's looking at."

"And what are you looking at?" Carl asked.

Staring at the window as if he could see through it just fine without the spyglass, Clint said, "That's Les. I couldn't tell you exactly what he's saying to those men in there, but that's him all right."

Carl studied the house for another few seconds before muttering, "I'll be damned. How the hell did I not pick him out before?"

"There're a lot of big men with guns in that house. Come to think of it, I may just know what they're planning in there."

"What's your guess?"

Rather than weigh in too soon, Clint asked, "Have there been more men gathering here as more days have passed?"

"They've been drifting in, but I couldn't tell which were new or which were ones I'd already seen."

"Have you followed them anywhere else but here?"

"Most all of 'em have been going to Pace's, but never together. They usually head into town after dark, so I figured I would just show you how they ride in and out."

Clint glanced up at the sky. There was some time before it became dark, which would give them a little while to scout a bit more. Even so, he said, "My guess is that these men are planning on robbing Mister Pace blind, and Les intends on leading the way."

FORTY

"Are you sure that's Les?" Carl asked. "I mean, it could be him, but it could be just about anyone under that hat and scarf."

"It's him," Clint replied. "He wears those same guns all the time and he always keeps his hands in that spot so he can get to them. Besides, it all fits."

"What does?"

"Everything I've been hearing. Everything you've told me. Bank robbers do the same thing when they're scouting out a place. They'll send their men in a few at a time at different times of day. And if there're a lot of guards or if the money's especially tough to get at, they may even raise some hell in or near the bank just to see how the guards respond."

"But if Les is down there, he would already know that. I worked at Pace's, so I know he's the main guard. Sometimes he's the only guard. He knows all there is to know."

"What about the money drops?" Clint asked. "Mister Pace trusted you to take the money to the bank. Did he ever send Les along with you?"

"No. He said he didn't want folks to know when the money was headed out."

"Maybe he didn't want Les to know either."

Suddenly, Carl's eyes grew wide and he lost some of the color in his face. "Jesus, I should've known something was going on. Why didn't I think of any of this?"

"Because you're a hardworking man who keeps his nose down to do his job. I've seen more than my share of robbers plying their trade," Clint explained. "After a while, it gets to where I can spot them from a mile away. They sniff around like a pack of timid coyotes for a while before they ride in. After that, they bare their teeth."

"Maybe we should let the sheriff know about this," Carl offered.

Clint took the spyglass back and looked over the old farm once more. "Actually, I thought there was a chance I might find DeFalco or one of his deputies among these men."

"So we're on our own?"

Although Clint didn't spot any of the local lawmen right away, he didn't cross them off his list of possible suspects. "Not necessarily. If I'm right about what they're doing, I can think of one man in particular who'd like to know about it."

Without any hesitation, Carl said, "Mister Pace! We can ride in and warn him. Les may be his main gunman, but he's got others who can help us."

Carl was ready and raring to go, but Clint wanted to stop him before he got too fired up. "Not just yet," he said. "If there's even a slim chance that my guess is wrong, we can't go in and light a fuse like that. We need to be more careful."

"But if we wait too long, more people could get killed." Making a fist and gritting his teeth, he added, "George is down there. I may have been too afraid to go in there before, but there're two of us now. We could take them by surprise and—"

"And nothing," Clint cut in. "We won't do a damn thing until we know what's going on. So far, all we've seen are a bunch of armed men gathering at an old farm. They could just be protecting George for some reason. Les might be his cousin."

Carl looked at Clint as if he'd just heard a bunch of gibberish come spewing from his mouth. "George is a wanted man. He's a killer. What else do you need to know?"

"Don't get cautious mixed up with fearful," Clint warned. "What time do they normally head into town?"

"A couple hours from now. Give or take."

"We'll use that time to do some more scouting. If they all head toward Pace's as a group, we'll know they're making a big move. Otherwise, they're just scouting some more for themselves."

"We can circle around this farm, but there isn't much more to see," Carl told him. "And the more we move, the better chance we have of getting spotted. You may recognize outlaws when you see 'em, but you're not the lightest man on your feet."

Unfortunately, Clint hadn't carried himself well enough that day to dispute the barbed comment. "We're still waiting until it gets darker. In that time, we circle that farm and then pick out a spot to dig in until sundown. Since we don't have numbers on our side, we'll need every advantage."

"And what if George decides to run before that?"

"Then," Clint replied earnestly, "we put him down like the murdering dog he is."

That was good enough for Carl.

FORTY-ONE

Carl was right about one thing. There wasn't much else to see while circling the farm. The old, crumbling structures were just as crooked from one angle as they were from another. Even so, he took Clint around in a careful path that Carl had obviously walked a few times himself. Along the way, Clint picked out some good spots that looked down on most of the areas of the farm that were being used.

All this time, the men in the farmhouse and barn didn't do much. A few came and went between the two buildings, and one even made the treacherous climb up the remains of the windmill once the sun began its slow crawl toward the western horizon. Having spotted George more than once inside the farmhouse, Clint had been content to wait for the perfect moment to move in. But when one of those men got situated in the perch of the old windmill, he knew his time was drawing short. With a man using that kind of high ground, it wouldn't take long for Clint and Carl to be spotted.

"All right, Carl. Remember that spot I told you about?"

Carl nodded. "The one just over there to the east. I remember."

"Take your rifle over there and be ready to cover me. It

may be a bit early, but we need to be ready in case that lookout up there catches sight of us."

"May not be as early as you think," Carl said. "Take a look."

Clint looked at the farmhouse to see a row of men emerging through a large hole in the front wall. That hole was big enough for the men to use it to lead their horses outside, which made for a very peculiar sight. One of those men was Les, and the fact that he'd been away from Pace's for so long didn't set well with Clint at all.

Watching for a few more seconds, Clint was able to pick out one important detail. "They're not all leaving. This works out perfectly. You stay put and get ready to use that Winchester. I'll cut them off before they get too far away."

"You'd better hurry. They'll be riding off before you know it."

"I know, and I intend to meet them when they're not thinking about anything other than snapping their reins."

"Should I start shooting when you do?" Carl asked.

"Not unless the men still at the farm try to get away. If that happens, just try to keep them pinned down. Shoot around them. Keep moving. Shoot some more and move some more."

Carl grinned. "Make 'em think there's more than two of us out here?"

"I taught you well," Clint said. "Even if you hear shooting, stay put and do what I told you."

"What if you need me to come help you?"

"Don't worry about that. Until I come back, we're both on our own. If you want to do this together, that's the way it's got to be. If you've got second thoughts, you'd better tell me right now."

Since the determined fire in Carl's eyes only grew, Clint kept low and hurried back to where Eclipse was tethered.

FORTY-TWO

Clint only had to keep his head down for the first portion of his run. Once he was down a small slope and past a clump of trees, he was able to race back to Eclipse at full speed. He barely broke his stride before pulling the reins free, jumping into the saddle and tapping his heels against the Darley Arabian's sides.

Now that he wasn't as worried about drawing attention, Clint was able to let the stallion run as if he was free to roam wherever he pleased. Sharp senses and keep instincts allowed Eclipse to navigate the uneven ground that was so far from any beaten track. There were a few close calls, but Clint made it back to steadier terrain before pushing his luck too far. When he found the trail, Clint stoked Eclipse's fire a little more.

Within a matter of seconds, he caught sight of the men riding ahead of him. There were four of them in all. Les was at the head of the group and he looked like a giant sitting so tall in his saddle. A short Indian wearing buckskins and a long coat rode beside Les. He was the first one to notice Clint racing to catch up to them. The way he turned in the saddle and effortlessly adjusted his weight showed that he'd probably been riding a horse since the day he was born.

The man at the middle of the group was a lean fellow who'd allowed his hat to flop off his head and hang by the string looped around his neck. He swapped a few words with the Indian and then turned around to get a look at Clint. When he did, the long mustache hanging down past his chin fluttered like tattered sections of a flag being flown at half-mast upon his face.

The fourth man in that group was Jerry, the bartender from Pace's Emporium. Clint may have been expecting a few others from that place to lend Les a hand, but he hadn't thought the skinny fellow would hang up his apron to take part in anything like this. If Clint had any doubts as to the intentions of any of the four men, they were washed away when the skinny fellow with the mustache drew his pistol and fired a shot at him.

Clint reflexively ducked and reached down to pull the modified Colt from its holster in a smooth motion. He brought the pistol up, tapped his leg against Eclipse's side, and steered off the path without taking his eyes from the small group of riders ahead of him.

The group stayed together until Les barked a few choppy commands at them. After that, he and Jerry continued down the trail while the other two broke away to circle Eclipse from separate directions. Clint swore under his breath. He'd been hoping they wouldn't be quite so prepared for visitors.

Before any of the other riders could get too set in their current paths, Clint pulled back on his reins and brought Eclipse to a near stop. That way he could see where everyone else ahead of him was going. After sizing up the others, Clint snapped his reins and got the Darley Arabian moving again.

The lean rider with the long mustache had split off to the right of the trail and slowed down to let Clint pass by him. Since Clint wasn't about to race into that trap headfirst, he fired another shot at him and tapped his spurs against his horse's sides. So far, he was the rider Clint worried about the least.

The one that bothered Clint a whole lot more was the Indian. After veering off to the left of the trail, that one had all but disappeared. Clint could hear the rumble of the Indian's horse's hooves against the ground, but couldn't quite place where he'd gone. His closest guess was still somewhere to the left, so Clint decided to head right and take out the more eager of the first two to come at him.

All Clint had to do to spot the man with the mustache was listen for the next gunshot. He didn't worry too much about getting hit, because if any man was good enough to knock him from his saddle while Eclipse was galloping that fast between all those trees, Clint was a dead man anyway. As expected, the other man's shots made a lot of noise but didn't do much else.

Like any good teacher, Clint followed one of the same lessons he'd passed along to his student. If the man with the mustache was willing to keep pulling his trigger, Clint let him do it. He counted every shot and moved in once he knew the other man was out of bullets.

Unaware of his predicament, the mustached man actually smiled when he saw Clint. "There you are," he grunted. "Picked the wrong bunch to follow, mister." He pulled his trigger, only to get the metallic slap of metal upon metal. To his credit, the man with the mustache was quick to holster his gun and reach for the shotgun hanging from his saddle.

Right about now, the Indian circled back around to race up on Eclipse's flank. Just as Clint had feared, the Indian one was a skilled rider with one hell of a fast horse. He got to a good spot and was about to put a quick shot through Clint's chest when he was taught a lesson of his own.

There was always someone quicker.

Clint pivoted in his saddle and squeezed his trigger. If not for the erratic motion of the horse beneath him, Clint would have put an end to the Indian right there. As it was, his bullet ripped through the skin along the Indian's face. The real damage was done more by the glancing impact of the hot lead against his jaw, which snapped the Indian's head around as if he'd been punched by a professional boxer.

The Indian twisted around from the force of the passing bullet, but still managed to hold on to his reins well enough to keep from being thrown. Clint looked to the other side and caught a glimpse of a shotgun in the hands of the man with the mustache. Without taking the time to give that man a full glance, Clint crossed his arm across his body and fired a shot into the shotgunner's shoulder. Although it wasn't a fatal wound on its own, the force of it did a real good job of sending the man with the mustache tumbling from his saddle. Clint heard the snap of the man's neck clear enough, even with the pounding of all those hooves around him.

When Clint found the Indian's horse riding not too far away, he thought another one of his problems had been solved. But the Indian hadn't fallen or jumped from his saddle. Clint realized that quickly enough when he saw the Indian's hand was still wrapped around his saddle horn. A thin leg was tucked neatly against the back ridge of the saddle, which meant the Indian was merely hanging off the side of his horse to use it as a form of living cover.

Clint fired a few shots over the top of the horse, which did nothing whatsoever to rattle its rider. Unwilling to deliberately shoot a horse just to get to a man hanging off its side, Clint tapped his heels against Eclipse's sides and pulled his reins to the left. He hadn't come this far just to put on a riding show with a redskin.

Before he got back onto the main trail, Clint had to dodge the few shots taken by the Indian. The first hissed a few inches past his head, but the second raked along his right arm like a hawk swooping by to shred through his sleeve with its claws. The next two rounds after that merely thumped into tree trunks, so the Indian saved the rest.

Les and Jerry weren't about to stay behind to help the other two. They'd been whipping their horses into a full gallop while Clint had been trading shots with their partners. Having spent so much time over the past few days waiting around or following someone else's lead, Eclipse was more than ready to hit a trail with everything he had. The Darley Arabian tore up the distance separating him from the two ahead of him in no time at all. All Clint needed to do was hang on for dear life.

Jerry turned around and nearly jumped from his saddle when he saw how close Clint had gotten. He said something to Les before taking a rifle from his saddle boot and levering in a round. Since Jerry had to stay on the back of a racing horse while taking his shot, Clint was content to bet on those shots missing their target. Instead, Clint turned to get a look at the trail behind him.

The Indian was closing the distance quickly and firing his pistol along the way. Those shots started off too close for comfort, and drew closer with each consecutive pull of the trigger. Clint pulled back hard on his reins so Eclipse turned to the left while coming to a stop. The move was quick enough to take the Indian by surprise, but smooth enough for Clint to maintain his balance.

Clint took a fraction of a second to steady his arm as the Indian thundered toward him. When he fired, he did so as if he was pointing his finger at his target and willing it to drop. Just to be certain, Clint emptied his cylinder and began reloading while the Indian was still reeling from the lead he'd caught.

The Indian fell from his saddle, but had the agility needed to tuck his chin against his chest and break his fall somewhat with his arms and legs. Even though he didn't snap his neck upon impact, he hit the ground hard enough to break something. Clint saw the Indian arch his entire body like a bow and groan as he lowered himself flat onto the ground. One arm was curled awkwardly and one leg looked to be twisted, but the Indian would live to ride another day.

Clint finished reloading his Colt, pointed Eclipse's nose in the direction Les and Jerry had gone, and then snapped his reins. He'd already caught up to them once and he was confident he could do it again.

FORTY-THREE

Carl's spot was marked by a thick cluster of tall trees situated just outside of the old Blair Farm's property line. The remains of a barbed-wire fence were only a few steps ahead of him. Beyond that, he could see the entire broken-down spread. Since the tree created a big enough silhouette against the horizon, Carl stood with one shoulder against it to steady his aim. When the gunshots began echoing in the distance, the old farm sprang to life.

The lookout that'd climbed the old windmill turned to look in the direction of the shots. Several figures emerged from the house to get a look, as did one of the men posted just inside the main door of the barn. Carl watched them all as if he was studying a big painting hung on a wall in front of him. He barely had to move his eyes to take in the entire scene. All he cared about was that the men didn't try to offer any support to the ones Clint was chasing down.

If those men knew what was good for them, they'd just stay put.

Naturally, those men didn't know what was good for them. They also didn't know anyone was watching them.

When one of the men ran toward the barn, Carl fired a shot that landed a few paces outside of the barn's door. The man who'd been running let out a yelp that Carl could hear all the way back from where he was standing and then drew his pistol.

Carl levered in another round and spotted more movement in the house. Someone was trying to lead his horse out of there, so Carl fired into the wall at the corner of the building. His shot didn't come close to drawing any blood, but it had the desired effect of forcing the man and his horse to duck back inside.

The man who'd tried running for the barn fired in several different directions. He spun crazily upon the balls of his feet, looking for a target and shouting threats to the surrounding trees.

Standing there with his rifle against his shoulder, Carl felt as exposed as if he was in the middle of an open field. He wanted to duck behind the tree, but was too frightened to move. So far, his inability to move had served him well, and none of the men at the farm had narrowed down the exact spot where the rifle shots had come from. If Carl stayed still, he might just slip their notice altogether.

That plan lost its appeal when two more men poked their noses out of the farmhouse. Carl couldn't tell which of those was George, but he could hear the man's familiar ranting.

"Bastard's in them trees! I can see him!" George hollered.

Carl flinched when the next volley of shots came, but none of them was pointed in his direction. Pistol fire crackled through the air and not one piece of lead hissed anywhere near Carl's tree. He smirked as three men inched their way out of the farmhouse. Carl fired a few shots, working the Winchester's lever as quickly as he could in between each one. George emptied his pistol, firing wildly in the wrong direction, but the other two men managed to narrow down their choices.

There were a few muzzle flashes from within the house

as some of the men shot through the windows. This time, Carl did hear the angry hiss of lead coming his way. When the shots got closer, he moved around to put the tree between himself and the farm. That was enough for the men in the house to find their target and the next few rounds started hitting the tree itself.

"Damn coward!" George shouted as he fired toward Carl. Rather than switch to rifles like the other men, George merely reloaded his pistol and used that. Fortunately for Carl, the pistol's range wasn't even close to long enough to be a threat to him.

Carl reloaded the Winchester and gritted his teeth as the gunshots kept coming. He could run away from the tree, circle around, and easily get back to where his horse was waiting. From there, he could escape from the farm before any of those men came after him.

But Carl couldn't let himself do that. As appealing as it was to simply leave the fight, he'd come too far to turn back now. Even if nobody knew it was him firing those shots, or that he'd skinned out when he had the chance, Carl would know.

Letting out his breath, Carl peeked around the other side of the tree and dropped to one knee, just like the soldiers he'd watched during the war. Carl sighted along the top of the Winchester and sent a round into one of the farmhouse's windows. He worked the lever, shifted his aim, and then fired at the barn's loft, where he knew a lookout was hiding.

"Same tree!" the man perched upon the old windmill shouted. "Same tree where he was before, but other side!" After that, he brought a rifle to his own shoulder and took aim.

Carl fired at the windmill and hit a spot slightly lower than where he'd intended on placing it. A bit of dust was kicked up from the bullet and a plank swung loose. That plank hit another one, which sent a creaking moan throughout the entire structure. The man at the top of the windmill grabbed on to it with both hands and struggled to find a better foothold. Since he was preoccupied, Carl shifted his aim from the windmill to the farmhouse.

Shots were being fired from the house in a slow, steady rhythm as the men inside adjusted their aim. Each time a bullet thumped into the ground or chipped at a tree, it was closer to Carl than the ones that had come before. Clint had told him to keep moving, but Carl couldn't get his legs to follow through on that. The longer he stayed in one place, Carl knew the chances of him getting hit would only get better. Since he couldn't get himself to move to another spot and he wasn't about to run away, Carl pressed up against the tree and steadied himself as best he could.

George was still shouting obscenities and firing his pistol angrily. Still the same loudmouthed jackass he'd always been.

When Carl saw that son of a bitch, he saw the only reason he'd gotten involved in this whole mess. He saw the man who'd killed his friend. He saw a man who didn't deserve to draw another breath.

Even though Carl was well outside of that idiot's range, he shifted his aim to the center of George's chest.

With one pull of the trigger, Carl could put that asshole down for good.

Then he remembered what Clint had taught him.

He had to squeeze the trigger, not pull.

FORTY-FOUR

Clint knew he could have caught up to Les and Jerry before too long. Unfortunately, they had just enough of a head start that he would be halfway to town before meeting up with them again. If the other two men knew a shortcut or managed to stay ahead of Clint for a little while longer, they might get all the way back to town where they could hole up in any number of spots. They might even have backup waiting for them there. Although Clint wouldn't mind taking his chances against those odds, Carl's odds would be a whole lot worse on his own.

Turning around and letting those two slip away went against Clint's grain so badly that it almost hurt. He set that aside quickly enough when he heard the sounds of gunshots coming from the farm. Clint snapped his reins and got back there as quickly as Eclipse could carry him.

The shots were getting closer. They cinched in around Carl like a noose, forcing him to lie flat on the ground and cover his head with his hands. He'd heard a lot worse during the war, but he'd been a kid back then. He'd seen men die, but still never thought it could happen to him. Only grown-ups bled that way and never got up again.

He was a grown-up now and he knew he could be dead at any second. Once that certainty hit him, the rest didn't seem so bad.

Carl forced his eyes open and checked his rifle. If he was going to die, it wouldn't be due to a lucky shot fired into the top of his head while he was lying on his belly. If these were his final minutes on earth, he'd spend them firing back at the son of a bitch who'd started this whole mess.

While thinking along those lines, the crackle of gunfire faded away. Carl no longer paid attention to the bullets that whipped past him like angry insects. He pulled himself up, lifted his rifle, and took aim at the men who were making their way from the farm to finish him off.

Clint charged from the trees and rode toward the farmhouse like a one-man cavalry battalion. The man perched at the top of the windmill fired at him, but Clint fired right back. He'd only meant to force the lookout to duck, but the boards beneath the man's perch had been weakened and he fell from his spot to drop at least twenty-five feet to the ground. He hit with a loud thump and let out a pained wail. Of the four men rushing toward the trees, two of them turned to see what had happened to their lookout.

Upon seeing Clint, one of those men brought his gun around to take a shot at him. Clint aimed from the hip, using nothing but raw instinct, and blasted a hole through that one's heart.

The second one who'd turned around fired wildly while launching himself through the air to one side. His shots were so wild that they wouldn't have hit their target even if it had been the old barn.

Dropping to one knee, Clint straightened his arm and fired.

When the man hit the ground on his shoulder, he was already dead. A fresh yet messy hole started at his chin and ended at the upper portion of the back of his skull.

Since the other two that had been running toward the trees had stopped by now, Clint walked forward and came to a stop where one of the dead men had come to a rest. "You up there, Carl?" he asked.

George stood facing the trees, but was nervously glancing back and forth between them and at Clint. "Yeah, Carl," George said. "Stick yer cheatin' head up for me."

Suddenly, Carl stood up and lifted his rifle to his shoulder. "Nobody cheated you, dammit!"

At first, it looked as if Carl was going to shoot George right then and there. Instead, he shifted his aim slightly to a point just over Clint's right shoulder. Before anyone could say or do a thing about it, Carl pulled his trigger, worked the Winchester's lever, and fired again.

The air became heavy and still.

Then, from behind Clint, someone grunted and hacked up a painful breath. Everyone else was looking in that direction, so Clint took a quick glance for himself. He was just in time to see another rifleman standing at the upper window of the barn. By the looks of it, he'd been about ready to fire a shot into Clint's back. The rifleman doubled over and fell head-first from the loft to the hard ground below.

Clint snapped his head back around to watch George and the last remaining gunman. "What the hell is going on here?" he asked.

"You're breathing your last breaths," George said. "That's what."

"Les talked you into helping him rob Pace's?"

"I don't know what the hell you're talking about."

"If you were a better liar, you'd be a better card player," Clint pointed out. "Since it seems like you're not good for much of anything, we'll just have to put you and your friend down for good so we can be on our way." With that, Clint sighted along the top of his barrel and Carl did the same. Fortunately, that was enough to get their point across.

"We were supposed to rob the Emporium, but that's over now," the man next to George said.

George wheeled around as if he meant to kill his partner on the spot. "Eckhart, you fucking asshole!"

Eckhart might have been at the wrong end of several guns, but he seemed more annoyed with George than anything else. "For once in your goddamn life, will you shut the hell up? We don't got enough men to do the job now anyway!"

"We still gotta try! You saw what he did to Paul."

Trying to get back into the conversation, Clint asked, "Who's Paul?"

"Paul's the man Les gunned down in the street," George snapped. "You should recall that, since you was there!"

Clint nodded as he remembered Les killing one of George's partners after the tournament. "If you're working for him, why would he do that?"

"Hell, I wasn't working for the son of a bitch until he did that!" Blinking as if he'd just sobered up, George said, "He came to me when I was locked up and told me I could either go free and help him or die. He swore that if I wasn't hung for what I done before, he'd finish me off the moment I was set loose. Since that lazy prick Sheriff DeFalco practically eats from Mister Pace's hand, I knew there wouldn't be anything stopping him from making good on that claim."

"So once you were out, Les put you to work for him?"

George nodded and finally let the gun slip from his fingers. In the space of a few seconds, all of the fight had drained out of him like water through a crack in a bathtub. "He said he intended on robbing the Emporium, but needed to clear out a few troublemakers that might make it tough for him. Delilah was one of those."

"What?" Carl growled. "You came in there to kill her?"

"Don't feel bad," George said. "I meant to kill you first."

"Why kill any of them?" Clint asked.

"Because Delilah had the goods on everyone at the Emporium. How do you think she was able to run her crooked game without bein' tossed out on her pretty little ass? She knew Les wasn't really backing Mister Pace, and when she got close to a known gunfighter like you," George said as he leered at Clint, "that was it for her. Les wasn't about to risk her being a thorn in his side."

"Why rob the Emporium?" Carl asked.

Eckhart chuckled and asked, "What else in Trickle Creek is worth robbing? Even the bank don't carry half the cash as what can be found in Mister Pace's office. The only reason he ever deposited any money there was to make folks think he kept it somewhere other than under the floorboards in his office. You really think he'd trust his money to a—"

"That's enough, Eckhart!"

The booming voice didn't belong to George, Clint, or either of the two men they held at gunpoint. It belonged to the towering figure that stood like a statue that had been erected at the edge of what used to be the farm's largest field.

FORTY-FIVE

Les stood in his familiar way, with both hands held within easy reach of the double-rig holster strapped around his waist. His back was straight as a board and his head was angled forward like a bird of prey examining mice running along a canyon floor. His lips barely moved when he said, "You shouldn't have come back here, Adams."

"I wasn't about to leave Carl to have all the fun," Clint replied.

"I'm talking about this town. This county, for that matter. You shouldn't have come back after the tournament."

"Is that when you decided to rob Mister Pace? You saw all that gambling money come in and you had to have it for yourself?"

"I been setting this up for months. Pace thinks I'll guard his money like a damn dog and get paid nothing but table scraps. That prick pays me less because I sleep upstairs from his precious saloon. After all the skulls I've cracked and all the men I've shot for him, he still ain't made me a partner. It's time for me to take what he owes me."

"Yeah! Me too!"

"Shut the fuck up, George!" Locking eyes with him until

George slumped over again, Les said, "You got two options, Adams. Either ride with me into town and help me tear up that Emporium to get Pace's money, or I kill you for the blood you spilled here."

"You're not in much of a position to make threats," Clint pointed out. "The only two men you got left are in a bad spot." Then, he noticed Jerry still on horseback near the farmhouse. The barkeep had a rifle to his shoulder, but Clint had to ask, "You think he's good enough to hit both of us from there before we clean out the rest of you? That's a lot of faith to put in a man who wipes up whiskey for a living."

"I don't need any help to kill you and Carl," Les said. "I face worse odds when I gotta tell a bunch of ranch hands to stop groping whores. You seen me work, Adams. Don't be stupid."

"You killed Delilah," Carl said in a shaky voice. "Robbing a rich man is one thing, but killing a good woman is another."

"She wasn't a good woman," George snarled. "She was a whore and a cheat!"

Carl bared his teeth and gripped his rifle tight enough to whiten his knuckles. "Shut your mouth!"

"Eh, to hell with all of you!" As he said that, George stooped down to snatch his pistol up from the ground.

Having already aimed his rifle at George, Carl twitched and pulled his trigger.

Clint knew he had about half a second to do something before Les cut loose with both of the guns he carried. That was just enough time for him to snap his arm around and fire as if he were pointing his finger at his target. The modified Colt bucked against his palm and sent its last round through Les's forehead.

The big man stood in his spot with a gun in each hand and not enough life in him to put them to work. His eyes rolled back into their sockets and he fell over like a tree that had been chopped down.

But Clint knew he wasn't finished. His Colt was empty and Eckhart was still unaccounted for. Clint turned to get a look at the last gunman to see if he'd actually made a smart choice. Instead, Eckhart raised his gun hand so he could burn down everyone in front of him.

Clint dug his toe under the gun that had been dropped by one of the men who'd already been killed, flipped the gun up into his hand and fired a shot. If he hadn't been standing so close to Eckhart, there would have been no possible way he'd hit him. Even at point-blank range, Clint only managed to put a round through Eckhart's ribs. That was still enough to take the fight out of him, and Eckhart crumpled.

George was already on the ground and Carl stood over him.

"You killed Delilah," Carl said. "Now you've got to pay."

George had been hit by Carl's first shot but was still drawing breath. His shirt was soaked with blood and he was on his back, but he simply refused to stop talking.

"Go . . . fuck yourself," George grunted.

"No," Carl replied. "Fu—"

"Carl. Don't."

He glanced up at Clint, but only for a second, and he didn't let his rifle stray from its target. "You heard him, Clint. He killed Delilah and it wasn't even an accident. He's got to pay for that."

"And he will," Clint said, "but not like this." He reached down to take the gun away from George. "He's unarmed."

"I don't care," Carl replied.

"And he's wounded. It's over. It took a hell of a lot to stand up and do what you did. I wouldn't have tracked them here before it was too late. If you weren't here, the rest of these men would have surrounded me and then ridden in to finish what they started. You did everything right so far. Don't stop now."

Carl just kept shaking his head. "I can't let this pass."

"It won't pass," Clint assured him. "We'll finish this the proper way. You pull that trigger and it'll just be an execution."

"That's what he deserves."

"Yeah," Clint replied, "but you don't deserve to have something like this weighing you down for the rest of your life." Although he knew Carl was listening to him, the sight of George's ugly, sneering face was counteracting every last one of his words. "Do you really think you'll be able to go back to a quiet life with this on your conscience? Once you cross this line, there's no going back."

"All these men crossed the line," Carl said.

"And they're not going back," Clint pointed out. "Trust me, we'll make sure of that."

After a long couple of seconds, Carl let out a deep breath and lowered his rifle. The moment George started to say something, Carl shut him up by slamming the rifle's stock against his chin. Finally, George was silent.

"What now?" Carl asked.

Clint smiled proudly at the other man and said, "Now, we bring the ones that are still breathing into town and hand them over to Sheriff DeFalco. There's a reward coming for George, you know."

Now, Carl smiled. "That's right. There sure is."

"Then we stop in to have a word with Mister Pace. After all we've heard and seen today, I think we can convince him that his guard dog wasn't as loyal as he thought. The sheriff may be a lazy ass, but Mister Pace won't be content to let these two get away with shooting up his place and trying to rob him blind."

Carl nodded with the confidence of a man who knew he

would see justice done. "Come to think of it, I may have heard someone mention that George was the one who'd been in cahoots with Les from the beginning. I bet that'd rile up Mister Pace even more."

"Yeah," Clint said as he looked down at the poor bastards curled up on the ground. "I bet it would."

Watch for

BAD BUSINESS

336th novel in the exciting GUNSMITH series
from Jove

Coming in December!

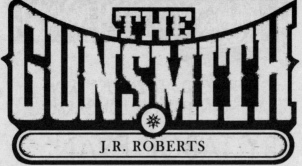

J.R. ROBERTS